BAD
VIBRATIONS

LUCY LEITNER

Interior Layout by Lori Michelle
www.TheAuthorsAlley.com

Cover by Deividas Jablonskis
www.dvartstudio.com

Printed in the United States of America

First Edition

Visit us on the web at:
www.bloodboundbooks.net

Also from Lucy Leitner

Part 1

"Blind acceptance is a sign of stupid fools who stand in line."
—Sex Pistols

Chapter 1

The woman with more chins than teeth asks if I'm here to see the cult. Yeah, she's the type to use the C-word. The type who are OK with living in this world that's killing them, eating all the poison, breathing in all the toxins, bleeding energy by the minute. Might as well be walking corpses. Just like Doctor says: they don't get it. In a society that does its best to make us sick, they'll demonize the only true way to achieve optimal well-being.

The invitation said this was unfriendly territory, but unfriendly can't stop truth. Detractors and deniers can't stop the awakening.

"I'm here for a wellness retreat."

"With the cult?" Her voice is gruff, but there's no stale cigarette smell on her diner uniform. Maybe she's among the ones that fear-quit during the early days of the virus. Takes a pandemic to knock sense into some people. Or maybe the voice is due to vices unknown to people who take responsibility for their health, who don't deny the dangers of modern life. Aren't smokers supposed to be svelte anyway? Maybe it's not smoke. It could be processed food, booze, factory-farmed meat, parabens, aluminum deodorant, lead paint, radon, tanning salon radiation, reheated cooking oils, car exhaust, leaf blowers, microwaved burritos, prescription meds, poor sleep, adrenal fatigue, leaky gut, fluoride in the water, or just not enough energy to keep all her cells alive. Takes a pandemic for even super healthy twenty-eight-year-old women with aggressive powerlifting and weight class goals and an organic lifestyle to see there's more that can be done with the help of the right doctor.

"It's not a cult, it's a movement."

"Heh," she snorts. "What's the difference?"

In the Instagram DM, @lululunges said to expect derision. They can't understand our discipline, our culture, our resilience. They're sleepwalking, she said. Wellness scares them, so they try

3

to shoot us down. We're threatening to dismantle the hegemony that's keeping everyone sick so they can't achieve their full potential. They laugh, chins jiggling, until they deteriorate into a hacking cough and phlegm and blood spatters from their mouths, soaking the surgical masks they still wear since they're never going to be resilient. But not in this town. Between the pickup trucks and ATVs in the yards and this woman's visceral fat you can see even under the diner apron suffocating her already deteriorating organs, it's more like the type of place where they stocked up on guns to shoot the virus. It's like they thought, well, we already have so much disease, what's another one going to do?

And to them, wellness is a cult. The routines we employ to keep healthy might as well be arcane witchcraft. Yoga, meditation, sharing each other's blood; the habits that keep us healthy people looking and feeling younger, to them, belong in a horror movie.

The blood is the life.

"You're vampires." The long, gray hair protruding from the mole on her primary chin flutters in the air released with the grunt.

It should be us giving them the sign of the cross! Reaching for garlic. Keep your diseases away from us!

"We're not vampires." How many times online and off does this need to be repeated?

"You drink blood."

"That doesn't make us vampires. Vampires suck the life out of their victims. We share each other's blood to share energy, to infuse new life into our veins. It's the secret to eternal health."

"We don't serve blood here. If you're gonna sit at my counter you're gonna have to order something." She shoves the menu across the tacky, stained plastic.

Ugh. The BPAs must already be seeping into my skin. @lululunges or whoever is giving me a ride to the ranch can't get here soon enough. At least the menu is paper. Thank Doctor!

"Is your produce organic?"

"Be more specific."

"Tomatoes."

"No."

"Cucumbers?"

"No."

"Carrots."

"No."

"Iceberg lettuce?"

"No."

"Do you know how long they have been disconnected from their roots?"

"What?"

"How long since they've been picked?"

"How the hell should I know that?"

"They weren't locally sourced?"

"I ain't gonna buy from your vampire farm, if that's what you're asking. If you are, you can get right the hell on out now. I'm sick of you parasites coming into my town and demanding I change my ways for you. I been here my whole life, been running my business how's I see fit longer than you been alive. Y'all got a lotta nerve trying to intimidate me into buying your vampire vegetables."

"Whoa! I'm not doing any of that! I'm just on a super strict diet. I'm gonna hit a 200-pound back squat by the end of the year while getting in a 57 kg weight class. I'm not gonna meet my goals if I don't eat super clean."

"So what do you want?"

Fries sound good. Yeah, they're trucked in from some commercial farm and cooked in oxidized oil. Oh the free radicals! But at least it's not animal flesh. It's not that level of energy draining like eating literal death. And this weekend will be filled with detox and fresh blood. If I don't meet my macros, it's OK. Calorie counting is not part of Doctor's prescription, just something I incorporate to meet my specific goals aside from highest possible vibrational energy. So, if I'm not in a deficit today, it only affects my competition goals. And no one has to know.

Unless whoever is meeting me at this free radical factory comes in . . . How much time before the others arrive?

"I'll take the garden salad."

"$3.50 ain't enough to keep me waiting on you in here."

"I'll take two garden salads."

"You'll take four or nothing."

"I'll take four."

"Doesn't make up for the business I lost when y'all put that 'poisoner' sign outside."

"I don't know anything about a sign."

"You'll take five salads."

"Okay I'll take five. We're not all bad!"

She rolls her eyes and turns around.

"We just want the world to experience true health!"

She pretends not to hear me as she passes through the plastic sheets that separate the dining area from the kitchen. The thin, saggy skin, the wrinkles, and the frown lines make her look a lot older than her capable gait. They must not have collagen powder in Caroline, PA. It's not like they have much else. That's how Doctor got the land so cheap. A full farm and all those summer camp cabins for the dedicated patients who made the move from LA. The sacrifice. They must have seen such tremendous results from the Practice. Like Andromeda, Doctor's wife, sick with the virus in the early days and rescued by her husband's blood after they'd tried everything else. Her life saved, her reason to live transformed. It worked for her when she needed it. It saved her. It works.

If it can save a life, it should at least help me get to 12 percent body fat, bench press 120 pounds, and make six figures at the agency.

This weekend will make it happen. Full immersion into the Practice. This flirting with the diet and following along with the YouTube yoga videos just isn't getting me there quickly enough. I need the blood. It's the life.

The door of the tiny diner swings open. In this greasy spoon, in this opiate part of the state, the girl who walks in just makes you want to say, "You're not from around here, are ya?" Rhinestone cowboy boots give way to perfect calves, lean but shapely, the kind some people are genetically gifted and others will never achieve no matter how many calf lift reps they perform. A flowered dress flows around the creamy tan skin of her long legs and her brown hair forms beach waves that my balayage would never achieve regardless of time spent with the curling iron. She's beautiful in an effortless sort of way.

She must drink a lot of blood.

"You must be Valerie!" She extends a hand. No thought that I may be infected. Just offers me her hand, the first such gesture in what, two years? "I'm Miami."

We shake. The energy flows. Her vibrations are high. Hand contact isn't enough. We're both craving energy. That's why we're in this town that just sucks the life out of you. It's been too long since a proper embrace. Energy can't be shared without some intimacy; sorry, Dr. Fauci.

We hug. Her vibrations pulse into me, mine into her. Miami, the beautiful Miami, filled with energy she's so quick to impart. My sister from this day on. Someone who understands.

We loosen our hold on each other, but the vibrations remain. We're each infused with the new energy created by an interpersonal connection. Not everyone exudes vibrations, as Doctor says. Some only have enough to sustain their own innate electrical systems and none to share. Others have achieved such high energy levels that they literally vibrate. They're the opposite of vampires; they offer their energy to you. Those who accuse them of being vampires are trying to steal their energy. It's ironic. It took me twenty-five years to understand the kids on the playground shouting, "I know you are but what am I?" were speaking the truth.

Everyone in the Facebook group says Doctor has the most intense vibrations, that he exudes them and can energize anyone in a six-foot radius. You can social distance and still be healed!

Miami takes the stool next to mine.

"So, I just have to ask everyone in the movement. Have you met Doctor?"

"No," Miami says. "But I'm so excited to. My friends—Medea and Mentor—they're meeting us here, they're longtime patients. They've met him a few times. They own a yoga studio in Cleveland. You'll love them. Medea had been diagnosed with all these health conditions. Then one day she sees Doctor on YouTube and starts following his protocol and BAM, she's cured. She's a beautiful soul. So is Mentor. He's so supportive of her. He started following the protocol too and it expanded his mind. They've been spreading the word in Cleveland."

"How did they get to meet him? Was it at an event?"

"I dunno. I never asked."

"You weren't curious to know what he's like?"

"Well, we know what he's like from all his videos. He's so authentic, not like the rest of the internet. And I heard he radiates vibrations. Ooh! Do you think he'll give us names? Like Medea and Mentor?"

"What would a name do?"

"Well, it means you're really a part of the Vibe. That you've officially become a new version of you. And you can leave that old, lesser you behind."

"What about *not* a new you, but a better *version* of you?" A you who can finally get a director title at an agency that seems to give them away quicker than Doctor gives his energy.

"I guess," she says. "But I know I'm ready for a new me. That's what it's all about, right? Leave the people stealing our energy behind. Get rid of all those things that take your energy. All the vampire foods, the stress, the low-vibrational people—all the things that keep you from achieving maximum energy. My name is stuck to all that old stuff that was killing me."

"Did you, like, memorize his speech?"

"I must have watched his 'What's in a name?' video like a hundred times!"

And it's almost like she didn't just smile back at me because that positive energy just evaporates as the waitress/cashier/cook shoves through the plastic partition that looks more like it should be in a carwash than a restaurant. The five salads are on the tray, anemic bowls of iceberg lettuce, matchstick carrots, chunks of slicing tomatoes, and cucumber wheels—none of which are fresh picked, their nutrients evaporated into the ether. Plucked out of plastic bags, these are neutral foods, according to the Protocol. They neither giveth energy, nor taketh away. They are acceptable substitutes when energy-bestowing, fresh foods are not available.

"Oh, great. You have a friend. Another Manson Family member?"

"Manson Family?" Miami asks with genuine confusion.

"She thinks Doctor's Prescription for Higher Vibrational Energy is a cult."

"Because we consider ourselves a family?" Miami asks.

"Because you drink blood."

"That's a small part of the Protocol. It's a holistic lifestyle focused on sustainable health practices for high vibrations and maximal energy," Miami says.

"OK, OK, what are you eating?"

"Is your coffee organic fair-trade Columbian?"

"No."

"That's OK then. I'll stick with the salad."

"The garden salad?"

"That's what this is, right? One for each of us and Medea and Mentor? And whoever is picking us up here? Thanks, Valerie!"

"Those are hers," the diner minder says. "You want to sit under my roof, you order something."

"Um, hmm." Miami's big, brown eyes scan the menu. Like everything else, her contoured brows are effortless and perfect like it all happened by accident and she didn't spend time in a salon with some angry Korean lady berating her for mangling her eyebrows when she should have been threading for years. "A cup of decaf."

"Ten dollar minimum for vampires."

"Five cups of decaf?"

The diner minder's arm flab jiggles as she grabs the full pot with the orange rim. It's 4 p.m. With the empty roads around here making it look like spring 2020, it's a safe bet that pot's been on since the morning. Can coffee oxidize? That Instagram ad I saw last week claimed a cup of coffee has more toxins than a cup of anything else we drink, that it's filled with pesticides and herbicides and mold and several other poisons. Doctor must not have covered that on any of his videos. The woman sets five white mugs on the counter and pours.

"I wasn't expecting them all at once," Miami says. "More like refills. One cup, five pours. I hate for you to waste the water washing all these extra mugs. You know water is a precious commodity. It's the current that provides all energy and should be cherished, consumed to fill us with life, never wasted."

"Cult minimum is now $15. What else are you having?"

"A garden salad?"

She turns and marches back into the kitchen.

"Doctor says it's them against us. They'll never understand, never truly accept that their way of life doesn't work. They're afraid of the truth," Miami says.

She pushes one of the mugs toward me. The porcelain is chipped. Mug raised, meeting hers, the mantra seems too natural coming out of my mouth. Do I really understand what it means? "The blood is the life."

The coffee is lukewarm and bitter, probably oxidized. Mental note to ask Doctor at the farm. Add to the list. Even so, the foul taste is an improvement over our diner minder's attitude. What's she so angry about? Her life must be so much easier; no expectations, no need to wear makeup, no highlights in her thinning boy-cut, no putting on a happy face when her world is falling apart. No clients asking why their website is delayed, why their ads aren't "resonating." No bosses demanding why the

Bad Vibrations

clients are calling. No one to please. Nothing to strive for. No hopes, no goals. It must be easier. But not great. Maybe she's satisfied with few teeth and aging skin and running a diner with a menu like we didn't just get a global wakeup call that our food is killing us. And maybe her life is easier being OK with it. So, why is she so rude?

The door swings open.

"Marigold!" Miami exclaims. The couple that walks in, they're not from around here either. "Banjo!"

The tall man and the woman, wearing what appears to be two masks, each hug Miami, but they don't share her exuberance. Something is wrong. They aren't vibrating enough for being on the Protocol.

"It's Medea and Mentor now. Remember, Miami?" the woman says.

"Oh, yes. So sorry, Medea. Is something the matter?" Miami asks, holding Medea by her silicone-gloved hands.

"We were followed," Mentor says.

"Not followed. Harassed. Nearly run off the road," Medea says. My salads can wait.

"What happened?" Miami asks.

"We were about thirty miles out on Route 85. One of those stretches with one lane in each direction. You can only pass when the sign says it's OK. There's a guy in this big-ass pickup driving erratically," Mentor says.

"Like a maniac," Medea corrects. Even looking like the Invisible Man behind the hat, sunglasses, and masks, she's the type of person who takes over a room. "Swerving all over the road. Inconsistent speeds. Like no one else existed. We needed to get out from behind him."

"So as soon as I could, I passed him."

"And that must have made his dick feel real small because he rides up about a foot behind us, starts flashing his lights, waving his arms, wailing on his horn, yelling god knows what. My lip-reading skills aren't all that great."

"That went on for like twenty minutes before we finally got a trailer between us and him."

"And we only got around him then 'cause he was distracted. He'd tried to toss a lit cigarette at us, but he forgot how wind worked and it blew right back into his window. It must've burned

10

the seat or something and he takes it out on us, starts giving us the finger and blaring the horn."

"Wow," Miami says. "Are you OK?

"We were just harassed by some lunatic who's as stupid as he is angry. He had a decal on the back of the cab that said 'Locally Hated.' We can't get to the farm fast enough." Medea hugs her shoulders like she has a chill in June. The tattoo on her arm says, 'The blood is the life.' She turns to Mentor. "That just stole all the energy you gave me this morning."

"I'm so sorry that happened," Miami says. "It's like Doctor says, most people just don't want to be well. And they go through great lengths to bring others down."

"I know the lecture, Miami. I got you into it, remember?" Medea finally notices me.

"I'm Valerie."

"I hope you had a better trip here," she says.

"It was OK. Uneventful."

"See Mentor? They don't want my kind here. Two white girls get here without incident and we have a maniac chasing us."

Mentor runs his hands through his long golden blond hair. It's got that slight natural wave my iron just can't imitate. "I don't like it either, babe, but he's gone. We lost him."

"Him," Medea says. "Not others like him."

The diner minder emerges from the kitchen, looking as dour as ever. Seriously. What is her problem? We've ordered the easiest items on the menu!

"Oh good. More. Like I told those two, $15 minimum."

"We're gonna need a couple minutes," Medea says as she pulls an antibacterial wipe from her purse and scrubs the seat next to Miami. She waves her gloved hand over it. Satisfied that it's either dry or sanitized, she sits down. Mentor rubs her back. That's sweet. They must have been together a long time, must make a lot of sacrifices for each other.

The now-familiar squeak means the door is opening again. The man that walks, no, struts in, he's from around here. He's not one of ours. Work boots, a white Hanes knockoff tee tucked into denim. A leather belt with a big, showy buckle. Buzz cut hair like he got turned down trying to enlist. A big grin. "Thought you lost me there, didn't you?"

Medea shivers. She keeps doing that, people will think she's having a bad reaction to that poison they jabbed us with three times. Well, me. They injected me before I knew about the blood, the antidote to everything. The others knew better and refused. They don't have to know about my transgression, my weakness, my fear. The rest were braver than I was, knowing the one thing they had to fear was an injection from those companies who profit on keeping us ill. Doctor says it's only a matter of time before they patent a cure for the sickness caused by their own vaccine.

Medea looks down at the counter. The man stares at the back of her head. He smirks.

"You know these folks, Royce?" the diner's one-woman staff asks.

"We haven't been properly introduced," Royce says. He sits at a table, kicks his feet up onto a chair like he owns the place. Maybe he does. Or maybe this is why he's locally hated. "We had a little incident on the highway and I was hoping they'd get the point of what I was trying to say to them. But now I see them in here, I see my point didn't get across."

"Oh, we get your point," Medea says without turning to face him. "You don't want my kind here."

"Bingo," Royce says.

"Sure it'd be a different story if it was just my man here in the car."

"Wait, you think we don't want you here 'cause you're black?" Royce looks shocked. The nerve. Then he laughs, the kind of laugh they make Halloween masks for. "You believe that, Edie?"

Edie grunts and shakes her head, chins jiggling.

"We've got no problem with blacks. Shit, we've got three black families in town. Elroy Johnson owns the gas station. Good man. Good kids, too."

"Good man." Edie nods.

"Nah, we got no problem with blacks here. Got no gripes with the homos neither. Asiatics, native folk, even those transsexuals. Hell you could be a cocksucking Chinaman who identifies as a flying squirrel and I'll buy you a beer down at Old Buckshot. Only people we don't like down this way is vampires. Right, Edie?"

"Right, Royce."

"We don't like a whole vampire cult moving into our town." Royce stands from the table. He's just a couple feet away. The stale smoke stuck to his clothes sends death into my lungs. The beer on his breath is worse. It's filling me not with death, but fear. Whatever he's capable of, it's magnified with booze. Hold my beer and watch me terrorize these city folk. "We don't like when your vampire cult friends come into town and start making demands. We don't like you brainwashing and poisoning our wives and daughters against us. So, I'mma be real clear now. We don't want you here. None of ya. And I'mma tell you right now that it'll be better for everyone if you got the fuck outta town now."

That's when he looks me in the eye. He means it. Hoping for a new name seems like a lifetime ago. We're in the now. Like the virus all over again. No future. No goals. Just surviving Royce.

The door squeaks again. Everyone but Medea turns. A young man, lean, arms covered in tattoos. All black ink. Symbols embedded in symbols. A life on the biceps.

"Just in time," Royce says. "You gonna pick up more victims for your bloodsucking cult? Or you gonna threaten to break dishes again if Edie here doesn't buy your hippie plants?"

"I'm here to tell you to let my people go," the tattooed man says.

"Why don't you take them out of town?"

"Why don't you see the truth, Royce?"

"Oh fuck, not this again."

"Some day you'll get it. You'll see that your drinking and smoking and driving around in your polluting truck is all just death. You, Royce, you're death. And someday you'll get why we chose life."

"Words of wisdom from a junkie," Edie says.

"Ex junkie," the tattooed man, who may or may not be here to save us from this toxin-filled, energy draining diner, says. "I told you my story to help you understand how our way of life makes recovery and rebirth possible. But you've chosen to turn a blind eye. Chosen to ignore the truth."

"And you've chosen to ignore this whole town telling you to get the fuck out."

"You don't want to start with us, Royce. You may not be used to it, but you're outnumbered here." Through the windows, behind the "Open 6 a.m. daily" painted on the glass, two gorgeous women stand in the parking lot in matching green, high-waisted yoga pants and sports bras and—are those bows and arrows on their backs? Athleisure for archery? It's supposed to be challenging, requiring zen master concentration. Maybe they just wrapped up a session with this guy. After all, he's dressed in the same shade of green. That must be it. They can't be security for a trip to a local diner.

"It's only a matter of time, freaks," Royce says.

"Let's go," the tattooed man says. We're ready; we all hop off our stools in unison.

"You're not walking out on your tab," Edie says.

Before any of us can reach into our purses, Mr. Tattoos shoves his hand in the pocket of his lightweight green gym shorts—the color identical to the attire of the two women in the parking lot— and tosses a fifty on the counter. He opens the door and we file out into the parking lot.

"Hey, Edie, the mouthy one's got a mask on!" Royce laughs.

"Didn't stop her from mouthing off though, did it?" Edie says as the door shuts, silencing any ensuing mockery.

Like Doctor says, they mock what they haven't awakened to understanding. It doesn't matter. They're practically dead.

Who cares what they say? They may as well be dead.

Chapter 2

Doctor says ingesting toxins after months of totally clean living can cause a weird bodily reaction that can sometimes mimic a drug, like when a legit keto dieter eats carbs. Did that cucumber poison me and I'm hallucinating some fantasy of @lululunges, one of Instagram's biggest fitness influencers, sweeping in with a crossbow to protect me from drunken haters?

When you don't have filters or perfect poses, not even one of your 800K followers could pick you out of a lineup of women all dressed in green gym wear. Until she gets closer and you can see the certain appendage that got her many of those followers and the endorsements that come with them and the life that looked so damn cool. The wellness retreats, all the elixirs made from saffron and other sorcery, the latest athleisure drops, the gorgeous apartment with enough space for home glute-building workouts during those dreadful months when the virus shut the gyms down, the experience with a naturopathic doctor-yogi in LA that made her realize the saffron elixirs and meditation app and keto diet were all just fads and the blood was the life. With the health nirvana she'd found, the acne she'd been airbrushing for years, the brain fog, and lack of purpose disappeared. Her endorsements for collagen potato chips and crystal chakra-balancing sleep masks and ovary-positive greeting cards rang hollow.

There was one truth: the blood is the life.

If you want to feel your best, achieve the you that you were supposed to be, you must watch DoctorEnergy on YouTube. Listen to his lectures. Pay $30 to unlock the diet plan. Donate on the website for daily guided yoga sessions.

They don't call them influencers for nothing. And what a time for @lululunges to share such wisdom, when everyone was stuck in quarantine, seeking better health to survive a virus that was taking out the weakest among us, those whose bodies were failing. Or just looking for a way to pass the time in isolation. Or both.

As soon as all these new followers were liberated, after Doctor pulled us through the dark months with hope and confidence and the most dynamic yoga practices to let all the frustration out, of course we'd sign up for the seminar. Finally! To be around people again! To meet my friends from the Facebook group and the in-app message board. To share human contact and blood. All that energy that for months was dissipating, draining every time you turned on CNN, accidentally read someone from an old life ranting on social media, contemplated turning an old shirt into a mask or toilet paper, feared the actions that just weeks prior were mundane the way Norman Bates made our parents' generation afraid of the shower.

But mostly fearing other people. The contagion, that evil among us. The people you love could kill you with their breath. Or worse, you could kill them. Trust no one, be alone. That's the only way to survive.

She gingerly places her crossbow on the ground to give me a hug. 2020 me would have never imagined that following @lululunges for her no-equipment glute growing tips when my gym was shut down would lead to me following her to this wicked little town for a weekend of drinking blood. Her hug is tighter than Miami's, stronger, from all her push-up and plank challenges, not to mention living full time on the farm with access to the blood. Hugging her back feels awkward, like I'm out of practice and forcing it. Not at all like the love and energy she's giving me.

"Welcome," @lululunges says when she finally lets go. "I'm Siren." Moving quickly, she picks up the crossbow from the ground.

I get it. After another day in this town, in the same zip code as Royce, I'd want a weapon too. Things are worse than I thought. This isn't the beginning of the story. We've walked into something rotten. It's like I'm finally seeing how the other half live. In my little bubble in the gym and online, I missed the hostility to wellness that I just witnessed in this diner where @lulunges said in her DM she'd pick me up. Obviously, Brad wasn't into the blood. If he were, we'd still be together. Or I'd have given up the only lifestyle that ever worked for me, and be frustrated again, stuck with another diet that stops my strength gains, another training program that fails to acknowledge my body composition goals, another mentor to let me down. More work, more deprivation, more struggling in pursuit. This, whatever this is with the energy and the blood, it works and it's the only thing that does. Yes, I'm used to Brad telling me it's weird and too intense and unsanitary and "anti-science," but he never had a visceral angry reaction to my journey or anything. Neither did any friends. We just lost touch when our lifestyles diverged. Nothing like the haters in the diner.

Our mission is even more important than I'd thought. This weekend will be amazing.

"I'm Valerie."

"No, you're not. You're you, so sublimely you, and we'll find exactly what name captures your essence."

"Siren. Weren't those the half-birds half-women who lured sailors to their deaths?"

"They were beautiful creatures with enchanting voices. The sailors couldn't resist their song."

"Didn't it kill them?"

"That's the conventional way of looking at it. That's what people in this dastardly little town would assume. But think of the life of a sailor in ancient Greece. Riddled with disease like scurvy, laboring under slave conditions. The sirens lured them to a better place where their energy was heightened and their souls aligned with heaven."

"Well, you lured me here. I'm actually kinda starstruck. Your Quarantine Booty plan got me through some dark times when my gym was closed."

"See? You've already found salvation from the call of the Siren. Doctor is so wise. And my name, like the others, pay homage to the Green culture where science and medicine blossomed. While some of our detractors may claim otherwise in their malicious attacks, Doctor's Protocol is pure science. It's been tested and tested, so we can conclusively say the blood is the life."

I nod, mouthing the words along with her.

Miami, Mentor, and Medea are receiving similar intimate greetings from the other bowhunter in yoga pants and the tattooed man. Outside the diner he's Mr. Rogers and it's suddenly a beautiful day in this bleak neighborhood on this main thoroughfare bisecting empty lots and shuttered buildings where businesses used to be. Maybe that's what you have to do to survive behind enemy lines. Surrounded by people who deny the existence of your truth. They're like the Israelis here. And these girls with their bows are Wonder Women.

"We should get out of here," Siren says. She offers to drive. "The backwoods roads out here are tricky," she says. OK, sure. No one's ever fought to drive the '09 Sentra. She doesn't comment on the empty Chipotle bags (from veggie burrito bowls, I promise!), the umbrella collection in the backseat, the bulk paper towels that will eventually make it into my apartment. I swear I have what it takes to attain optimal wellness! I'm just busy and no one was supposed to be in my car! She positions her crossbow on top of them and drives the Sentra with grace, and is forthcoming with information, unperturbed by the things giving me misgivings.

"Phoenix was a straight-edge growing up. I don't know a lot about it, but apparently it's punks against drugs. He became disillusioned with the movement and got into heroin. He found Jesus in jail, then lost him when he got out. Then he found Doctor and rose from the ashes to a whole new being, dedicated to ultimate wellness and defending our message and beliefs against all who try to bring us down," she says. "It's a beautiful story."

We're off the main road, past the old houses with the For Sale signs, boarded up garages, and a bar with a full parking lot. Somewhere in this blight is utopia? Yes, yes it is. That's why "diamond in the rough" is a saying.

Siren turns the Sentra down a gravel road, past a silo. The two mini-SUVs—Miami's and Mentor's—follow, their owners, like me, in the passenger seats.

"So, that guy in the diner . . . he really doesn't like us, does he?"

"Oh, no he doesn't." She laughs.

"I guess he is kind of a clown. Still, he scared the pants off Medea."

"Oh you get used to it. None of them like us. We represent everything they won't let themselves achieve. The virus didn't wake them up. They're still clinging to their wrong ideas that are killing people and themselves. They hate us because we're tearing down their illusions. But they're too afraid of the truth to come to the farm."

"Typical hater."

"You are so right! He is so out of touch with his own innate capacity for wellness that he says a lot of hateful things based on fear. Oh, you're going to love the farm! Such positivity. Everyone helping better one another, like a family. But better! It's a family we chose." She smiles at me. The family she chose over the ones that paid for the orthodontics. This must be an amazing family. One worth protecting?

"I gotta ask though—bows and arrows? That's not for like, self-defense, is it?"

"Oh! Phoenix caught us in the middle of a session."

"A session?"

"Oh, honey, you have so much to experience."

We ride in silence for a few moments, the first time to myself since before arriving at the diner. It's hard to process strange events with non-stop chatter in a language in which I'm not yet fluent.

The scenery is less depressing now that the despair of burnt barns, boarded buildings, and biker bars crowded way too early for socially-distanced social drinking have given way to farmland. Lush green crops carpet the rolling hills. Corn maybe? Wheat? Who knows? They're growing in abundance and that's what matters. If this is what Royce and Edie and company can grow, imagine what awaits at the farm!

"But what's the session?"

"Archery, of course!"

Duh. It's what Doctor calls 'dynamic meditation.' I've tried it while squatting, to let everything else melt away while focusing only on the task at hand. It was great until I forgot to stand up from the squat. Eighty-five pounds gets really heavy when you sit with it for Doctor-knows-how-long ass-to-grass.

"You've never felt such intense focus," she says. "The world just melts away. I was always seeking such concentration. They said I had ADHD. They drugged me for years and it turned out my parents should have taken me to the shooting range! Instead, they threw money at quacks with prescription pads and took me away from myself. I shifted my paradigm, see? Doctor says I'm still detoxing from decades of meds. I'm still discovering myself again. When I do, Doctor says I'll be ready for blue clothes."

Drugs again. Albeit legal, prescribed even. If she can achieve that radiance after years of ingesting poison, there's no way this weekend won't get me, and my twenty-eight years of clean living, to my goals.

"I've never done archery. That bow looks . . . intense." It's black, carbon fiber maybe? It looks like it's from after the apocalypse which, in a way, it is.

"Oh, you're going to adore it! I'd never tried before, as I said. I'm not really an athlete. Maybe that's why Mom and Dad went straight to the pills."

"I am. I was a college distance runner, high school track and swimming. Now I'm working to become a powerlifter."

"A powerlifter? Wow! You don't look like a powerlifter."

"I know. That's what makes it so difficult to accomplish my goals."

"It's a good thing," Siren says. "You look like a yoga instructor. And who doesn't want to look like that?"

"I guess. I could still be leaner, you know, to stay in a lower weight class and gain that advantage."

"Weight class? Like wrestling?"

"Yeah, pretty much."

"What weight class are you in?"

"I dunno. I haven't gotten that far yet. I've been plateauing in gains the last few weeks and I really don't want to do more of the auxiliary work at the gym. It's so boring and time consuming! Doctor's Protocol has been the only thing that's giving me any gains. I added five pounds to my squat since starting and ten to my deadlift since trying the blood at the seminar last month."

"I don't know what any of that means, but it's an inspiration. You're an inspiration. Phoenix is an inspiration. I'm an inspiration. We all are! We must spread this message and inspire others. No matter how much they resist!"

"Ten pounds on a deadlift isn't much of an inspiration. I was actually a little disappointed. I feel like it should have been more by now."

"You're heading in the right direction and that's what matters. Everyone else in this country is headed off a cliff." She smiles at me, like that was a reassuring statement. You're making slow progress while the rest of the world tries to drag you down with them. "And you have a lot of energy potential. Doctor will see such possibility in you."

"Harpy told me that at the seminar last month. How can you tell?" Kyle the agency senior vice president informed me yesterday that if I didn't exude more enthusiasm for a 2.8 percent boost in ROAS on our remarketing skyscraper ads on weekly status calls, our clients would never be persuaded to up their monthly retainer. One of them has to be wrong.

"The breasts are where we store our energy. It fortifies the milk we feed to our young. The bigger the breasts, the more energy potential. You have a lot of potential."

The road is barely a road anymore. The Sentra nearly exceeds its width and kicks up rocks that better not crack the windshield. The two SUVs trail close behind. A deer—they have deer in farmland?—runs into the road and Siren slams the brakes. Miami's Kona is nearly in my back seat.

The deer crosses and Siren proceeds with seemingly no difference in heart rate. Maybe the cornfields have a calming effect. Maybe staring at them long enough will make that happen. They are cornfields, right? Commodity crops, sprayed with poison and ground down to toxins we happily ingest by the truckload in the name of saving time and money, Doctor says. We've lost the ritual around food, the miracle of its gift of energy. So many steps from the Earth to us. The energy is pulverized and it fills us with toxins and fat. Doctor's farm can't be an industrial cornfield.

"You doing OK there?" Siren must have caught the cornfield thoughts on my face.

"I'm fine."

"Having doubts? It's OK. We all did. You're about to experience a lifestyle few will ever be so lucky to know. But I'm not going to tell you it isn't different. It is. Sublimely different."

"I just haven't spent a lot of time outside cities. And everyone is so . . . different from me."

"We're a beautiful mosaic. You'll see."

The cornfields give way to a forest, dense with trees of all types. The late-August leaves are full and green on the living trees. The many dead lay on the forest floor, skeletal remains of once thriving life, a microcosm of the scene in the diner, of America as a whole. The road turns to gravel as it snakes through the narrow path between the woods and Siren rides the brakes down the hill. It seemed odd at first, but thank Doctor Siren offered to drive. The directions would have been something like, "Pass your eighth cornfield then turn left at the oak that was struck by lightning in 1996." Let that be a lesson for the weekend. Everything has a rational, scientific explanation. And it's all for my own good.

Pop!

Chapter 3

It's not a gunshot. It takes a second to realize that. The Nissan skids down the gravel, suddenly unbalanced. Screaming. Is that me? Siren's knuckles are white around the wheel. The car stops. My heart is fluttering. It feels like there's no blood in my head.

Siren yanks on the wheel, but the rear feels like it's got a mind of its own, like it's on ice. When it finally stops, the Nissan is jackknifed across the road, barricading it.

Phoenix is knocking on my window.

"Are you alright?" he's shouting from the other side of the glass, his poker face from the diner now showing all the emotions. I nod. Was I telling the truth? I'm in no pain. There was no physical impact, just shock.

Siren's eyes are closed and she's breathing with the rhythm of a metronome. That seems like a good idea. Breathe in, one, two, three. Out, one, two, three.

"Siren, come take a look at this!" Phoenix shouts.

Siren snaps out of her meditation and practically jumps from the car. She runs around the hood to my side, joining Phoenix in examining the front passenger tire. Whenever I told myself I hoped the Nissan died so I could have an excuse to upgrade, I should have been more specific. A peaceful death of natural causes in its sleep. One morning, it just wouldn't start. Not a violent end in the middle of those small towns that the news, at least last time I tuned in, said was opioid country.

I join Siren and Phoenix and others with their mouths agape, staring at my tire. More specifically, a small wooden plank with two spikes embedded in my deflated tire.

"Damn. DIY, much?" Medea says, raising her eyebrows at the makeshift car deterrent. "I've never seen one of these so small."

"Or detached from the ground," Mentor says.

And they usually come with a sign that says "Caution: Severe Tire Damage," so scumbags don't just roll their trucks into a gated community.

"How am I gonna get home?"

"Oh, don't you worry about that!" Siren laughs. Her near-twin and Phoenix join. "We can fix it right up."

"I don't have a spare, only a donut. You can fix a tire?"

"Of course!" Siren says. "We are totally self-sufficient here."

"The local mechanics won't take our money. Anything we didn't already know, we taught ourselves," Phoenix says. "You been doing Doctor's yoga at home, you know YouTube's better than any school these days."

My heart slows down. It's not catastrophic. It's a flat tire. Happens to everyone all the time. The Sentra was a victim already this spring during pothole season, and it was all OK. Fixed by grimy men with cigarettes in their mouths, not Doctor's blood running through their veins. It'll be OK.

"But why would that thing be out here?" I ask.

"This thing?" Phoenix rips it out of the tire. I half expect it to make some dramatic noise, but the tire can't be more flat than it already is.

"The previous owner of this place was a bit of a loon," the other woman, still not introduced, says.

"Drunk," Phoenix says. "Liked to hunt on this land. Great combination. Shit. Last week we found a bear trap, isn't that right?"

The two women in green nod.

"My guess is he rigged this to catch something. Booze and eating death. No wonder he had to sell. He was weak. Squandered all of this."

Yes. This. The farm. Shangri La. So focused on the tire, I didn't look up. The orange sky accentuates the lush greenery ahead. Just yards ahead of the Sentra, a Prius and a Tesla are parked as the gravel ends in grass. To my right is more dense forest, but on the left, the trees form an arc around a line of a-frame cabins—like the ones that look so idyllic before the psycho killer arrives at camp—only interrupted by a perfectly appointed red barn. On the other side of a wide, baseball diamond dirt path, another line of cabins and a ramshackle ranch house provide a barrier to acres of farmland. The green crops, whatever they are, stretch back to the horizon in small, rolling Pennsylvania hills. Nothing in Pittsburgh is this green. Green grass, green stalks of some sort of plants. Reds of berries and tomatoes interrupting the green. It's like an exclusive golf course, but with a purpose. A fantasy. Emerald City. What farms never looked like but what our collective memory imagines them to have been. Utopia. $3,000 seems like a bargain for the privilege of seeing such natural beauty.

"It's beautiful," I say. "I've only ever seen this in puzzles."

Siren laughs. "Just wait til you experience it. Be present all weekend. Do not detach. You will be living in such beauty that your mind will be constantly doubting whether it is real. Just accept it. You've arrived."

"I'll take care of the car," Phoenix says. "You can head to the farm."

"I want to help," I say. "You guys are so self-sufficient and I totally tuned out when my dad tried to teach me to change a tire. That's part of the prescription, right? To be independent of anyone who causes illness?"

"Looks like someone doesn't want to wait for her grays," Medea says.

"You know, Valerie, typically Whites start with a certain set of tasks. Sweeping the barn, husking corn. Learning the most important, basic skills of the farm before advancing to the luxury tasks," Siren says. "But seeing how this is your car, I understand. And I am so appreciative of your initiative."

Initiative. That's what Blake, the agency president, called it after our presentation to the valve company. The one that just happened to occur right after the weekend seminar in which I first tried the blood. It was the blood that made me so assertive in the presentation, calling our digital marketing solution a 'panacea.' It was a high. Without any blood since, it's like I've been hemorrhaging the opportunities needed to make Director. Another shot of blood should be just what I need to take the lead and deliver on all the promises I made in the pitch meeting. Another shot of blood and maybe I can bypass white entirely.

"So, so impressed," Siren says. "We won't start the orientation without you."

"C'mon, I'll show you your quarters," the green-clad armed woman who is not Siren says. With their bags—not many, just backpacks and shoulder slings—Mentor, Medea, and Miami follow her toward the orderly rows of cabins. Onto those greener pastures where they'll find out what they can be. It's just me and Phoenix now, the man who became all that he can be after apparently burning his life down. He inspects my tire. He fingers the plank but doesn't extract it. Would be it like pulling a pin from a cartoon bomb?

"You really drove all the way out here with a donut and no idea how to get it on your car?"

"I've never been so far out AAA won't be there faster." I pull my phone out of my pocket, like he can't figure out what I mean by calling. No bars. "Or that I can't call AAA."

"You weren't prepared," he says, squinting at me, protecting his eyes from the setting sun.

"I guess not."

"You know, I wasn't prepared. My whole life. Fuck, man, I thought I was. Didn't come from much so I fended for myself. Got in with one crowd, but couldn't make it work. Got in with another, a real bad crowd. I wasn't prepared to make good decisions. Went to jail. Sure as shit wasn't prepared for that. Nothing prepares you to be locked in a cage with men so bad we got an armed force in every city whose job is to make sure you never meet them. It wasn't 'til I got here that I really got it."

"Got what?"

"How to live. This shit works. It's fucking out there—I know—but it works. I'm calm. Content. No fucking drugs or shit either. Where you keep your jack?"

I pop the trunk, remove my overnight bag, shove aside the old lifting belts and straps that did not help me get personal records and that I really need to finally list on Poshmark or just throw out, and dig out the jack that hasn't been used in at least the past three years that I've owned the car. I pull out the shiny wrench that sat in the cardboard box next to it as well. It seems I was paying attention to at least part of the lesson. Do better this time. Be present like Siren said. This is all part of the experience. The healthiest people on Earth can take care of themselves. We don't need your injections or your chemical creations you call food or your "help" that's just designed to make us dependent for more. We have everything we need.

As Phoenix pumps the jack, the car slowly lifts. He attaches the wrench to the lug nuts on the wheel and tugs. Nothing happens. He stomps on the handle, but even putting all his force into it, the wrench doesn't budge. He stands on it. Nothing.

Bad Vibrations

"Looks like the nut's rusted," he says.

"So, you can't fix it?" My heart starts pounding again. Be present. Be present. Don't think about the risk of missing work on Monday.

"Of course, I can fix it. I just need some more energy to get this thing off."

"Maybe I can do it. I'm training to be a power lifter."

Phoenix laughs. "You're low on energy too." He looks at me right in the eye like he's looking through me, into my brain, into my soul. People don't look at each other that way, not even when eyes are all you see above the mask. What does he want with my soul?

"The diner, the people, the whole town, just driving through it felt toxic on a metaphysical level."

He nods, like he understands whatever just came out of my mouth. "You need energy."

"It would make me feel better." He gets it. Ex-druggie knows the fix. "I feel like this may have been a step backwards."

"It's not. Not with the right infusion."

"You got some blood to spare?"

"Nah, that's tomorrow. I'm talking sex." He's still looking into my soul, but now his hands are on my hips. It's not like that drunk guy at the bar or the party who can't hear no. It's not sloppy, not lustful the way his fingers grope, the way his body pulses against mine, all while his eyes keep staring into mine. It's not sexual, even though it's about sex. Spiritual?

"I wanna give you my energy," he whispers in my ear. "Do you want my energy?"

Energy? Yes? His? The tattoos, the crowded teeth, crooked face filling in some of the details of the stories told by lines in the taut skin. So many lives lived in such a short time. He must be barely older than me, yet accumulated so many more years. The wiry build, the buzzcut only slightly concealing the receding hairline. Energy? Yes. His? Eh.

Phoenix's lips are on mine. His bulbous tongue fills my mouth, sliding around slowly like it's exploring rather than kissing. Yet somehow for all its weirdness, it feels good. His hands slide up and down from my thighs to my ribs. That feels good too. The energy is already seeping into my body.

But as he removes his hands and opens the back door of the Sentra, it's gone. The vibrations cease. He beckons me in.

"I can't do it. Not in the back of a Nissan. I want to sell this thing this year."

"The surroundings don't matter," he says, quite matter of fact, like he's lecturing on western civilization, not propositioning me. "It's about the people. Look around. We were in Southern California, but we made fucking Shangri La here. You'll get it when you reach optimal energy. Where you're at don't mean shit."

"When I reach it. For now, I can't even get into a state to receive energy in the back of a used Nissan with a busted tire."

"Suit yourself." Phoenix pushes the door shut. "Hit me up when you find a place where you'll get in that state."

"OK."

"Grab your bag. I'll get Archimedes to help me get the tire off. You've got orientation anyway."

Chapter 4

Siren tells me to leave my bag on the stoop of my cabin, the first of four on the side of the clearing that abuts the woods. She and her green twin, who finally hugs me and introduces herself as Calliope, lead Miami and me, and two new Whites, Shane and Faylor, down the dirt path. They've all changed into their whites. Yoga pants and a sports bra for Miami, just like our two guides. Loose white pants and t-shirts for Shane and Faylor.

"Aren't you gonna change into your whites?" Shane asks me.

"She will after the orientation. It's important to see the farm before the sun sets."

"Sorry, I couldn't take the time from work to get out here earlier."

"We understand," Calliope says. "Not everyone can make the commitment to this lifestyle as we have here, to abandon our toxic, energy-draining jobs in pursuit of wellness."

Uh huh.

"I just don't get the clothes," Shane says. "I mean, I'm sponsored by the most comfortable athleisure brand in the world. You've got some massive social media firepower here. I could hook us up." White wires attached to nodes stick out from the low neck of his tank top. He hasn't told us the story behind those yet, but if the five minutes with him so far are any indication, he will soon. And he'll have a discount code.

"The colors signify our energy levels. White means a newbie. You may feel the best in your life, but understand, there are far higher levels. You also have yet to shed your dependence on the outside world—like heart rate monitors as an indicator of wellness," Siren says, nodding at Shane's wires. "Grays, like Medea and Mentor, have spent weekends with us, but are yet to make the full move to settle here, so their energy depletes every day they are away.

They prepare the food that we have farmed and support the security of our little paradise. They can attain our green status by demonstrating their ample energy in recruiting more members, spreading the energy to more curious people like yourselves, or supporting the ranch in ways that can only be possible by heightened energy. Phoenix is so close. We support the operations of the farm. Organizers. While we love our work, we strive every day to earn our blues. The Blues handle the blood. Athena and Io are both real medical professionals—did you know that? Athena is a psychiatrist and Io a nurse. Both traditionally trained and finding their skills are better suited here. Since they've attained optimal energy, they get the honor of relaying Doctor's message to the outside world."

"Like on YouTube?" Miami asks.

"Yes!" Calliope says.

"How have you been doing that with no service here?" I ask.

"Oh, we have internet in Doctor's house where he lives with Andromeda. Only when you have attained such high levels of energy can you live with such temptation. The internet is a toxic place. As greens, we have to manage our access very carefully. That's why we make appointments to post to our followers just a few times per week from the house. For Grays and Whites, the toxicity depletes your energy too quickly. You must accept that you will have no access to the outside world for the duration of your stay this weekend."

"No problem," Shane says. "I go dark once a month anyway. No social media for three days. Ayahuasca instead. Clears the mind."

Doctor's house is little more than a shack in desperate need of a power wash. If it were covered by overgrown weeds and anywhere else, local kids would dare each other to enter, see who was brave enough to face the ghosts. Once-white aluminum siding covers the entire single-story ranch home, only interrupted by curtained windows and a front door aligned too far to the right for comfort for my symmetry-loving brain.

"The interior is brand new, renovated to maximize the energy potential of each room," Calliope assures us as I observe the red paint peeling off the door. She must notice because she says, "It's taking a while to complete since we're working on a special non-toxic paint. You would be aghast if you knew how much blue matcha butterfly pea powder it takes to pigment enough paint for a house!"

The barn, directly across the thirty-foot-wide or so dirt path, dwarfs the shack both in height and prestige. Even when constructing paradise, you need to prioritize to get the work done.

"The barn is where we imbibe our energy," Calliope says. "The blood as well as the gifts of the farm."

"What are those exactly?" I ask. "Siren said we husk corn, but it looks like that's not all the crops."

"Oh yes! We grow tomatoes, blackberries, kale, all manner of squash," Calliope says, waving her toned arms at the vast field. Farmer strength. Functional. Maybe that's what I need to break through the 160-pound back squat plateau. "You'll experience the joys of farm labor, of hard work with your entire body, on Sunday. Tomorrow is all about energy acquisition."

Energy then gains. Makes sense.

Our tour turns around as the edges of the field obscure into darkness. The Greens bid us goodnight, Faylor and Shane walk to their cabin across from ours, and I pick up my bag from the step, finally entering the small, yet elevated A-frame cabin. Ours is the first cabin in the clearing, on the side abutting the woods. Two sets of bunk beds, one on each side of the room, leave about twelve square feet of open floor. It's not sleepaway camp; it's everything Fyre Festival pretended to be. The walls are that light maple like you see in ultramodern flooring, smooth, not the rustic logs of a Unibomber cabin. Essential oils provide aromatherapy from the tiny windowsill of the tiny window a few feet from the front door and the bay window on the back wall gives us a view of the dense trees and brush, growing darker by the second as the sun sets. Weighted blankets cover the beds that somehow embrace you so all the weirdness of the day can just melt away. Almost.

"There's no bathroom in here." So, the essential oils are not to mask the smells from a too-close toilet.

"That's what the woods are for," Medea says from a bottom bunk where she sits with Mentor. I toss my bag on the one across the tiny room as Miami hurls herself on the bunk above me.

"You can shower in the woods?"

"Oh honey, what year are you living in?" Medea asks. Her masks are finally off, so it's easy to tell that she's judging me.

"Valerie! All these abrasive soaps and hot water damage the skin microbiome!" Miami says, slapping an oversized hand on her undersized thigh. "I think that was video 194. Your skin microbiome is responsible for warding off pathogens! And everyone's just out there scrubbing it off! Leaving themselves open to all the viruses, just inviting them in."

"Where do we wash our hands in the woods?"

Miami, Medea, and Mentor look at each other like they're my parents and I just asked where babies come from.

"Honey, you don't want to scrub off your immune system on the part of your body where you need it most," Medea says. "That's how you get diseases."

We sit in silence, my head down. Hopefully they're seeing shame that I didn't watch all 438 or however many videos on Doctor's channel and not shame that I may not be ready for this level of commitment. Is that it? Am I hesitating again? You gotta commit. That's what coach Trevor said. If you really want to get good at powerlifting, you can't be thinking about physique all the time. You can't be scared that you'll get fat and lose your cardio fitness because you're just lifting all the time. It's not working because you're not committing, he said. Sneaking in eight-mile runs before work and burning off all your gains. Who knew you could fail to commit and overtrain at the same time? Who pays $3,000 to come all the way out here just to repeat the same behaviors that failed before? Not me. I will never attain optimal energy if I don't follow the whole prescription. If that means outdoor toilets, that's what I have to do.

"Your journey is clearly just beginning. Don't you trust us?" Madea raises her eyebrows. Somehow she manages to keep them raised while glaring at me. We're all sitting on our beds like it's summer camp and she'll make me streak as a dare if she deems my response untruthful.

"I do! I trust all of you. And Doctor. I know I've got a ways to go, but I'm in such a better place than I was before. It's just . . . "

"It's just what?" Medea leans toward me like she's playing the bad cop with no good one at her side.

"It's like the people in this town, like the virus didn't happen. They're still eating the same crap, living same toxic way. They didn't learn! Meanwhile all of us here, we've been doing it right all along and we've made a pilgrimage here, paid all this money to be even better. And that drains my energy because no matter how well we become, it'll just keep happening again and again."

"Those who don't learn from history are doomed to repeat it," Mentor says, like he's in my brain.

"There's a gap between us and them for sure," Miami says.

"It's a fucking abyss," Medea says. She's still frowning, but her glare has softened to something like empathy.

Silence. Just the fireflies outside. Like living in a white noise machine. Then a wail. A scream. It's instinct to run to the door. Yeah, run toward the screaming, toward the danger, like running upstairs when the killer bursts through the window. The others follow me out the door, down the single step. The residents of the rest of the cabins have the same idea. We're a curious bunch. That's why we're here.

The corral between the rows of A-frames is empty, the people in white and gray and green milling around when Phoenix brought me down here went away with the sun. The only sounds are nature. Then another scream, wailing in agony.

"Should we get someone?"

"For what?" Mentor asks.

"For whoever that is who's in pain."

"We're all in pain. That's why we're here," Medea says.

"No, I mean he sounds like he's in real, immediate pain."

The scream pierces the calming nature sounds again. It's louder now, like it's getting closer. From the darkness, a figure emerges in white. It stumbles in front of the big, red barn on the opposite end of the ranch as where the poor Nissan is waiting for surgery. The figure—who appears to be a man, from my vantage point at least, clad in loose white pants and a white t-shirt like a mental patient—stops and lets out the longest, loudest, yet most strained and crackling wail yet. Two other figures, women it seems, in much darker, tighter attire grab him by each arm. He buckles at the knees, and they drag him back into the darkness, out of sight, away from the cabins.

"Show's over," Medea says, turning back into the cabin. We follow.

"What was that?"

"In order to attain the highest level of energy, you must free yourself of all the toxins—physical and mental—that are weighing you down," Miami says. "That can be painful."

"That didn't sound or look like someone freeing himself."

"You're really low on energy," Miami says.

Medea claps her hands. "I know! Do you like dick?"

"What?"

"Men, do you like them? Or women?"

"Men. I like men."

"When was the last time you had one?"

"What do you mean?"

"Sex. When was the last time you had it?" Medea asks. It doesn't feel right revealing such personal information to someone whose full face I've only just seen.

"That's really not . . . it doesn't matter."

"Aw, she's nervous. Yeah, you're right, Miami. Low on energy."

"I'm not nervous. It's just. Well, I just met you guys. This is a little personal is all."

"Honey, if you can't tell us that, you're not gonna last long here. You gotta commit, or this whole protocol for wellness isn't gonna work for you. We're family here. You can't tell me when you last got dick? That's like lying about your medical history here. You can't get a prescription without an honest assessment of where you're at."

"I—"

"Five times a week minimum," Medea says. "Are you getting it five times a week? That's the prescription. Are you getting it?"

"No."

"Do you want to be?"

"Well, yeah. But I'm single. It's not an option, is it?"

"Of course it is! Mentor's right here."

Mentor smiles from his perch on the top bunk across from mine, like he's reminding me that he's here.

"I can't do that. He's your boyfriend." And he's lanky with long, scraggly hair and not really my type.

"Husband," Medea says.

"Even more can't do that."

"Why not? It's just energy. He's given his energy to Miami so many times when she's running low."

"Mentor's really good at giving his energy," Miami says. "His touch is electric. And it gets better from there."

"I'm like a battery," Mentor says. He hops down from the bunk and sits next to me. His hand is on my back, rubbing it. He smells like a hedge. This may be the first time I've ever thought about an aroma being part of my type, and his is certainly not. He traces his fingers on my quads. He must not notice how underdeveloped they are. His touch is soft. It feels good. He wraps his arm around my back. Stroking my other leg, leaning his face in with his hawk-like nose and breathing into my ear. He's gentle, like Phoenix.

"Oh, shit. Mentor, you need protection," Medea says.

"I can't do this."

"Why not? You have to. It's your first step toward optimal energy," Miami says.

Medea reaches into her bag and tosses something gray to Mentor. He stretches the gray fabric over his face, covering his mouth and nose. The face mask says "WELLNESS" in white block letters.

"I can't in front of you."

Mentor apparently can. His hand has moved into the waistband of my joggers. Who knew you could get two propositions in one day wearing glorified sweatpants? He appears to be kissing my neck, though it's hard to tell under the mask. His soft breath is a warm, wet breeze in my ear. So much for the mask keeping it inside.

"Did you hear that?" Medea asks.

It's hard to hear much with Mentor's canvas-covered tongue in my ear.

"It sounded like a car," Miami says. "Maybe more people are coming. They must have heard the good news."

"Honey, that may not be a good thing."

A car horn blares, loud and long, then a few short beeps before a sustained wail. No alarm makes a series of sounds so random. Mentor leaps off the bed to the door. He cracks it open and peers outside.

"Come on out, vampires. We've got a present for you," a voice slurs.

How did someone that drunk get his car down that winding road? Why is that my first thought right now?

"It's that asshole from the highway," Mentor says.

"I knew it." Medea shakes her head. "They've gotta keep asserting their dominance over the one part of this town they can't control."

"Y'all better come on out. You're gonna really want to see this," a less slurred voice shouts.

It's two drunk rednecks in the pickup truck that likely has the indisputable phrase 'locally hated' on the back window. None of us needed to come out to see that. We could have guessed it. Royce stands in the bed of the truck that is too shiny to have ever been used for truck purposes other than being an asshole on the highway. Maybe he'll fall over the edge and land on the other moron who is standing on the grass. The high beams blind the shirtless guy who peers out the door of the cabin across from ours, hiding his eyes in his elbow like a COVID sneeze, then he shuts himself back inside. Blinding your audience, quite the way to get them to look at what "we're really gonna wanna see."

"We don't like you freaks here," Royce shouts. "We don't like your bloodsucking and your big city diet food and that weird screaming. And we don't like these either." Royce raises a hula hoop over his head. "These are for little girls. And little boys who like girly shit. Not for you."

"Not for you," the man on the ground echoes. "You can't just take over our town. We ain't standing for your abducting our children no more."

"We're here on our own free will!" a woman screams from somewhere on our side of this weird standoff.

"Ain't that what that rich lady—that one who robbed the banks..."

"The fuck you babbling about, Wade?" Royce asks.

"You know who I mean. Rich lady kidnapped by some *simians* or something. Wound up robbing banks with them."

"You're making that up. I never heard no crazier shit in my life."

"This lady's real. It happened a long time ago. They took her and she wound up on their side. Pamela something. Penny, maybe?"

"Patty Hearst!" The name just comes out of me, at a volume I didn't know I could summon. The track coaches always said my lungs were my ticket. Medea covers her ears. For emphasis, apparently. She turns and glares at me.

"Patty Hearst!" the moron Wade says.

"I'm sorry, it was hurting my brain."

"Well, now it's hurting my ears," Medea says and turns back to watch and wait to see just what Royce is going to do with that hula hoop. Maybe attempt to straighten it.

"Never heard of the bitch," Royce says.

"They say it's like she was brainwashed into thinking her kidnappers were her friends."

Bad Vibrations

"Well, that sure is a good story, Wade. Can we get on with it now?"

"My bad, Royce. Your show."

"Now if we ain't made it *a-buntly* clear. We want you brainwashing vampire fuckers outta our town. So take this—" He raises the hoop in one hand while lifting a spray bottle in the other. While trying to coat the entire ring with whatever is in that bottle, he drops the hoop three times. Why doesn't he just vomit on it? That would no doubt be as flammable as whatever accelerant he's fumbling around with in the truck bed. Hasn't everyone by now figured out he's about to burn a fake hula hoop in effigy?

Finally the lighter is raised.

"This used to work for some folks down south, I hear," Royce says. "We don't agree with their politics none, but they sure as hell got the job done."

Wade grasps the ring and Royce holds the flame to it. They release and the flaming hoop rolls into camp. Just as it reaches the wide path between the two facing rows of cabins, it falls onto its side. The ring burns on the ground.

"You sick, narrow-minded loser!" A figure in white darts from the cabin across the small field, standing near the fiery ring. The person yells with seething rage. "Go back to your barstool. Drink your vitamin depleter and neuron killer. You may have set this hoop on fire, but it'll never be as inflamed as your organs."

Silence but the crackling of the fire. Then laughter.

"That the best you can do...uh...boy? Sweetheart? Not really sure what you are," Wade says.

"I'm someone with more energy in my duodenum than you've got in your whole body."

"Well I'm not sure having that body part makes you male or female."

"You look like a cytokine storm," another voice shouts.

"I bet you can count your natural killer cells on one hand," says another.

"You're so oxidized you might rust."

"You have so many free radicals it's like your cells just liberated a GULAG."

"If I put the world on an elimination diet to figure out what was causing the problems, I'd start with you."

"You're an irritable bowel."

"Your vitamin D levels are so low they're hanging out with you." That's my contribution.

"You think EPA is just the government agency."

"Your T cells are as diverse as your town."

Out of the cacophony of your mama type jokes, a chant erupts. "The blood is the life. The blood is the life. The blood is the life."

It's hard to hear beneath the chants, but it sounds like Royce says, "see you" then something else before he turns the ignition.

"You're complicit in a machine of death!" the figure in white screams as the truck swings around and growls up the hill. It's like the exhaust is spiting on us after all our critiques about free radicals. The hoop is little more than a ring of smoke on the ground. Miami joins the person in white stomping out the remaining flickers.

"Take off your mask, Medea," Mentor says. "Remember how the toxins stick to the fabric."

"Oh yes! Get it off me! Get it off me!" Mask off, she gasps for air. "Ugh, I can taste the reactive oxygen species."

"I know, babe. You need some energy?"

"Oh, so bad," Medea says. They retreat to the cabin and it's like freshman year in the dorms all over again.

Besides Miami and myself, all the others milling around the corral between the cabins are wearing some version of monochromatic workout gear. They watch the flames flicker from a distance, unwilling to get close enough to inhale the toxic smoke. They must not have a Mentor who can recharge any energy the smoke steals.

"I don't think there's any fire left," Miami says.

"I know. It just feels good to stomp those haters out," Faylor says. The voice is a little deep like a man's, but I think the point is for me not to be thinking about that. Or for me to be thinking about it too much. Like I am now.

"Can't they just leave us alone?" Miami asks.

"No. We're a threat to their existence. We challenge their conceptions of the way things are and they can't take it. Shane and I have met too many people like that, people who can't understand that we've moved beyond gender and that gender never really existed in the first place. They deny and deny and they lash out. These people are the same. They'll go so far to deny their way of life is fatally flawed."

"So, what do we do?"

"Fight back. You're not going to appeal to reason; they're too far gone in their own shit for that. They're not going to see things like we do. So, fuck them."

"That sounds a little aggressive," I say. "A little like them. Like we're throwing our own flaming hoop, fighting fire with fire."

"You ever tried talking to fire?" Silence. "Anyway," Faylor continues, "you heard Doctor's giving a lecture at breakfast?"

Miami and I shake our heads no.

"You'll really want to hear what he has to say."

Chapter 5

When you say "Doctor's healing powers" out loud, it sounds really stupid. That's what Coach Trevor said when I said I was moving on, that I'd found something that was helping my lifting more than all his years working with top squatters ever could. 'All doctors have healing powers,' he said. 'That's why they're doctors.' But Doctor can heal what others can't. He can heal things that other medical professionals don't even think needs healing. And he does it through his unique Prescription for Wellness.

He's not some faith healer or a televangelist charlatan. He's a real doctor. A naturopath.

Through his prescription, he has healed fibromyalgia, Hashimoto's, chronic pain, leaky gut, diabetes, adrenal fatigue, Lyme disease, and COVID-19. He strips the weight off the obese and gives it to the anorexics, he turns drug addicts clean. His Prescription does miracles the science way. He lives his Prescription, used it to attain the highest levels of energy ever known. He's inspired thousands—132K followers on Instagram and twenty legit disciples who have devoted their lives to the pursuit of energy and this ranch. He has the methods for fending off all that ails our species, and he shares them with anyone open minded enough to listen.

It's almost like he's attained such a heightened level of existence that he's surpassed being a pure human. No mere mortal could hold such powers to cure. If so, why hadn't it ever been done before?

And yet, when we're seated at our tables in the barn, waiting to bite into our carrot and apple breakfast, it's a man who enters. He's barely taller than me, and maybe even leaner. His light brown hair is streaked with gray and pulled back in a low ponytail. He's

Bad Vibrations

clean shaven, like the rest of the men here, and wears John Lennon style glasses without the smug shades. His baby blue button-down is tucked into his loose linen slacks, like he's a professional relaxer. All eyes are on him. All lips are sealed. No breath is drawn or released, like riding an elevator in the spring of 2020. There was no formal announcement; it's just what your instincts dictate you do when you know it would be frowned upon to scream and run after him like it's Beatlemania.

We're seated at long folding tables like at a redneck wedding. The colors segregated at each table give the large room a flag-like appearance. Blue, green, gray, and the white neophytes; Miami, me, Shane, and Faylor. The white capri yoga pants, white sports bra, and white crop tank that arrived on our cabin doorstep this morning came with tags from a brand I don't recognize, but that Miami assures me are "legit." It's one of two outfits, the other, similarly white and yoga-inspired, is presumably for tomorrow. We'll see. At least my $3k night of glamping now includes some new cute gym clothes.

Turning our chairs from the table to the makeshift stage gives us a full view. Even from the pulpit, he doesn't give the appearance of towering over us mere mortals seeking his guidance. He's on our level, at least physically.

Then he speaks.

"Family, it is with great displeasure that I tell you this, but it needs to be said."

Shit. Looks like I came just as the great wave finally broke and rolled back.

"We are at war. War with twenty-first-century life. The famine of real food forcing us to rely on processed, man-made, chemical, genetically modified, toxic plants; plants that should be a source of life and energy. The famine of feasting on death, the dead flesh of our friends in the animal kingdom. The pestilence that it unleashes. The death we've just endured.

"How much more? you ask. How much more chronic disease, pharmaceutical poison, suicide, addiction, pandemics, and 3XL t-shirts can a population endure before they realize they must change their ways? I had hoped our recent disastrous run with a virus would have brought more people to the light, but it has not. And we are not only waging a war against the lifestyle that makes us sick and anxious, drives us to drugs and medications, and leaves us susceptible to plagues. No, we are simultaneously at war with people who deny this truth.

"I didn't want this for us, but they're resistant to new ideas, ideas that prove their unhealthy, toxic way of life is killing them. The social networks block our posts. Their so-called fact checkers are just as deluded as the rest of them. The search engines bury our websites under the government agencies responsible for the food pyramid. They flag our videos as misleading; the mainstream medical drug dealers shout down our truth from their ivory towers. The media grandstands and debunks our proven healing, energy-sharing lifestyle.

"Even the people in this little opiate-ravaged town call us a cult. Vampires even. They deny what prescriptions did to their town. Like everyone else, they saw death from the virus. And they wore their masks and they locked themselves in their hovels with their TVs and their Schlitz and their Hot Pockets like they were told. But they didn't learn. They keep eating and drinking and smoking and sitting on their couches like it never happened. Never accepting, or even acknowledging that a healthy body free of toxins is impervious to disease.

"And yet you, my family, you keep pushing on. Because you're not going to succumb to the rapture of disease that will wipe out the rest of our country. Yes, that day is approaching. It will be soon. We just got a massive, global warning and we didn't heed it. Instead, we fought one another. We invented terminology; social distance, flatten the curve, anti-masker, super-spreader events. We took malaria drugs and wrapped ourselves in plastic and ran into traffic when another person passed. All to keep us safe from the virus. When all the while the best defense was within us. But most had been lulled to sleep and unwilling to follow the one true cure for any disease. A healthy, well lifestyle that makes a strong immune system.

"And that's why we must prepare for war; an existential, ideological battle between us and those who deny that truth. We will be vigilant and fend off all attacks on our way of life because that's what they are: attacks. By impassioned online defenses, or by bow and arrow. Whatever threatens to silence us, we will fight back. We will secure this ranch, this little hamlet where we thrive and reach the highest energy levels that we'll need for the war and what comes next: the complete devastation of mankind. While plague and chronic disease wipes out all who don't listen, we'll be here, thriving off each other's energy and the earth.

"Be ready, family, because Armageddon is coming. You're in the right place to survive it."

Doctor stops talking. The room comes back into focus. He gazes around the tables at all the young, lean, high-vibrational faces. We're all rapt. We got the message the virus sent us. Why the fuck can't everybody else?

"Now eat up! You need fuel for yoga."

The carrot on the piece of wood that serves as Miami's plate is maybe six inches long, but she's eating it centimeters at a time. A nibble, then she places it back on the plate before moving on to the cashews. She takes a bite, leaving two-thirds of the nut on the plate. The fruits, raw veggies, seeds, and nuts are like a cornucopia on our plates, overflowing in the abundance of the harvest, yet she still savors every bite like it's her last. Maybe she's thinking about the anemic produce from the diner. Yes, this is the Shangri La that will survive the apocalypse.

"That was enlightening," she says.

"He's right about the war," Faylor says, glaring at us from behind threaded brows and lash extensions. With the army-issued haircut, pouty lips, cropped t-shirt, and baggy sweatpants, Faylor presents a conundrum for anyone dependent on pronouns to describe a scene. Whatever. At least I'm not writing a book. "Those people in this town are desperate to start one, if last night is any indication."

"If that's the beginning of a war, it'll be a short, sad one," Shane says, biting the leafy end of a celery stalk. He chews, takes another bite. Oh. That wasn't a mistake.

"They sent a message last night. Burning hula hoop? Burning cross? How do you not see the similarities?"

"It didn't really make the statement they were looking for, did it? They're not that bright," Shane says, crunching, his mouth full of leaves and fibrous bits.

"People who burn crosses in people of color's yards aren't known for being smart," Faylor says in earnest. "That doesn't make them any less dangerous. They hate us because we're well, and they can't handle it."

"That may be true, but we can defend ourselves," Shane says. "We're on their turf, we're not exactly victims here."

"Of course you'd say that. You've never been a victim."

"Oh here we go." Shane rolls his eyes.

"You've always been accepted. You didn't lose all your Greek life friends from college when they didn't like your gay friends from the club. And you didn't lose all your gay friends when they didn't like your non-binary friends from the Facebook group. And you didn't lose your non-binary friends because they didn't like your Prescription. So, yes, Shane, I am a victim. But so are you. And the sooner you accept it, the better off you'll be."

"And the sooner you learn to deal with fear, the better off you'll be. You gotta do fear training. It'd help you out to get all this in perspective."

"Ooh what's fear training?" Miami asks. "Is that like skydiving or staying a night in a haunted house? Or getting an exorcism? Because I've done that."

"You've had an exorcism? The church still does that?"

"Oh no, it wasn't the church. It was a secular exorcism."

"Is it a private company? Would they exorcise me complimentary in exchange for a plug on the 'Gram?" Shane asks.

"I'm not sure," Miami says. "Do you have a demon?"

"I've got all the demons," Shane says, smiling at Miami. Looks like an energy transfer is imminent. He's not really handsome, but he oozes fitness and wellness and life, which are the only attractive things to ooze. "So anyway, I work with a company—solid people, they pay me, but I wouldn't endorse them otherwise—Petrifi. They deliver the ultimate bespoke terror experience. You go online, fill out the detailed questionnaire and one of their in-house, certified fear consultants designs a custom series of surprise frights designed to make you confront your deepest fears. You get chased by a deranged army vet who looks like your stepdad throwing live spiders at you on your way home from Pilates, you think of public speaking differently. Seriously, try it. Discount code SHANE20 gets you 20 percent off."

Faylor glares at Shane. Miami stares at him with rapt interest. Maybe she followed him before this weekend. Maybe the Instagram algorithm suggested an obstacle course racer turned biohacker known for his willingness to try anything that can optimize his life experience. Well, known to some people. Not me.

"I don't need to hire people to scare me when we're in the middle of enemy territory." Faylor takes a bite off a celery stalk, a snap in lieu of a mic drop.

Bad Vibrations

"Maybe if you used my discount code and booked your free fear consultation, you wouldn't be sitting here worrying about some rednecks."

"Well, I found Doctor's speech enlightening," Miami says. "And the whole world is trying to kill us, you know? With receipt paper and soybean oil and everything in between. So how much should we really worry about the people around here?"

"Well said, sweetheart," Shane says.

Faylor responds with an eye roll. Time for mine to close. The crunching of the carrot drowns out the argument at my table. Chew slowly. Slower. Savor each crunch. Listen to it instead of Shane. Focus on the crunch. Everything else falls away. The room is gone again. It's just me and the carrot, transferring its vibrations into my body. Straight from the earth, replete with natural energy, it seeps into me as the masticated carrot pieces slip down my throat, every one of them palpable. Nothing else matters. Nothing but the energy taking me to a higher frequency. Nothing—

"Yes, family, this is how you absorb maximum energy from plants."

Blinking my eyes open reveals a room of people staring at me, like that naked anxiety dream. Can Petrifi make that happen? The voice, Doctor's voice, unmistakable, right behind me. He leans down, his head nearly resting on my shoulder as he whispers in my ear, "Your energy is substantial. You'll attain great levels while you're here. You may be wearing blue sooner than you think."

My face is hotter than a burning hula hoop. A charge flows through my ear into my veins, tingling, flooding me with a lightness. Energy.

Chapter 6

The metal compound bow rests on my shoulder. It's the women's model. Lighter, or so they say. The way it feels really puts into perspective how far I am from my lifting goals. Maybe blue yoga pants are nearer my reach than a lifting meet. The color is more flattering in these sports bras and leggings than my whites; it concealed any excesses in the curves of those ladies in yoga class.

Focus. That's what the Blue said in the brief instruction before she handed me a weapon and pointed me at a target. Focus on your breathing. Or was that at trampoline hula hoop yoga? You have to focus on your breathing to have enough air to expel all the toxins in a primal scream as you bounce while swiveling your hips to keep that hoop spinning.

The bow sinks, the crosshairs now barely above the ground. Focus on your breathing to keep your shoulders even. Focus on your breathing to expel air to power out of a squat. It's everyone's advice. Is it a metaphor or can one really forget to perform an automatic function that keeps us alive?

"Remember to breathe." Doctor's own breath warms the back of my neck. My heart beats faster. Now I have to breathe to slow it down.

Inhale. Line the crosshairs back up to the head. The human outline on the target is an odd choice, but how often are your enemies perfectly round? And like Doctor said when we started this exercise in total focus, "When did a series of concentric circles ever mount an offensive?" But this isn't really about warfare, is it? All that talk this morning was figurative, right? There won't be a battle between the forces of good and evil. If there is a war, it'll be with information. The people who take bad advice will be the casualties while those who follow Doctor's truth will live to fight another day.

So, the arrows are that next level of mindfulness, requiring so much more concentration than the faster-paced, proprioceptive Primal Flow session. It's way easier not to fall off a trampoline while performing a hopping, hip-swiveling tree pose and unleashing a Sleepaway Camp scream than it is to aim this heavy bow.

"The scream releases mental toxins. Anxiety, anger expel from your lungs. And you replace them with energy you summon to unleash your primal cry," Doctor explained at the beginning of the Primal Flow class right after breakfast.

When you scream like that, you feel it in your whole body. It's not just from your throat. It can't be, not when you scream that many times. You'd run out of throat. It's from your gut, your abdomen, maybe even your soul. It rises into your lungs until you just have to expel it. Because it feels, well, toxic. And you have to exorcize the toxins. It's exhausting and gives you newfound admiration for the scream queens of horror movies. Screaming is an art, especially on the small trampolines. You need your lungs to move, to hold the poses while bouncing and keep up with the class, especially the Blues in the front who flow through the routine with ease.

Afterward you feel purified. You've screamed out most of the toxins, the ones that multiply because of your own damn neuroses. The rest you sweat out. The energy the modern world sucks out of you is restored.

Doctor led class, demonstrating each pose to its limit while still in his linen pants. We were all in our color-coded yoga attire. The two women who wear the deep, royal blue with the scrappy backs were front and center, taking most of Doctor's attention. The famous Andromeda, Doctor's wife and his first patient, with her full figure and lack of concern about staying in a weight class, sunk into each pose like she was water, kept her hips churning with the rhythm of waves crashing ashore. How could she hold her leg behind her head like that as the trampoline quivered while us Whites summoned all our energy to stay on one leg? The perfect hourglass figure, the gliding movements, the serene expression while she screamed like Jason just exploded out of Crystal Lake.

How could this be the same woman who the hospital sent home with an oxygen tank after nearly succumbing to the plague of 2020? She was one of the unlucky ones who got it early, when our marvelous modern medicine thought the only way out was shoving a tube down a throat and hooking a patient up to a machine. Their one tool, their hammer. Andromeda was one of the lucky ones whose husband knew better. His vegan, local produce diet and detoxifying yoga practice had already cemented his influence among a relatively small group of online acolytes as well as the patients at his homeopathic LA clinic. He didn't know what he knew, but he knew anything the goombah in New York demanded was wrong. The machine wasn't the life, the blood was. Doctor was desperate. Andromeda had an oxygen tank and vertigo. So, he pricked his finger and let her drink.

It wasn't a miracle. There are no miracles in science. But the next day, Andromeda was improving. So she drank again. And every day after that she drank her husband's blood, she had more life. Doctor had only a small Instagram account on which he shared Primal Flow and vegan recipes for optimal energy to a couple hundred patients. As he documented the blood journey on his account, his following grew. People were posting their Energy Prescription grocery hauls and tagging Doctor. Women were screaming on TikTok while they held camel pose. It became a viral trend, the screaming yoga challenge. A hula hoop shortage sparked DIY creativity that apparently spread to even our drunken neighbors here. The biohackers shared their shots of blood. Pre-workout or post-workout? That was the great debate. Silicon Valley executives were passing blood around before pitching investors. It was a nootropic, a stimulant, a purifier, the life.

The retreats were exclusive at first. It was like you needed at least 100K followers to get an invite to Doctor's new sprawling ranch outside of LA. With the prohibition of mass gatherings, they were the only events in the state. The attendees shared photos of the trampolines and testified to their rejuvenation. Everyone else was locked away in a perpetual rock bottom and there they were achieving optimal energy.

Spending months alone in my apartment, working to keep fellow housebound, anxious clients happy and workouts consisting of only air squats and pushups, my goals were slipping further away. By the time I got back under a barbell, a year of gains were gone, my energy with it.

Siren, who I knew as @lululunges at the time, wasn't drained like me. She was filled with life and energy in her posts. She was following Doctor's Prescription. If it was as effective as her

Bad Vibrations

equipment-free glute routines that brought me to her account, it was worth a try.

The yoga practice was easiest to implement. Even at the height of fitness equipment shortage, I could still find a mini trampoline on Amazon. And it's not like I had much else to do. The diet was tough, not because there was a run on veggies or anything, certainly not in Pittsburgh. But it didn't jibe with my macros. You can't get one hundred grams of protein from non-GMO, organic plants without blowing up your bathroom. Maybe I needed to be more strict and really adhere to it, but Trevor said that even my attempts to follow the diet were preventing me from reaching my goals.

You can't expect strength gains if you're starving yourself, he'd say when the gym finally opened back up. He just wouldn't get that it wasn't starving myself; it was starving out the toxins. Brad didn't get it either.

No matter what they said, what I was doing was working. For the first time since the world shut down, I felt like my life was moving in a positive direction. Weights felt lighter. I felt lighter. Not like for a weight class, lighter in spirit.

So when Doctor posted a list of all the seminars in the spring, I booked the East Coast one right away. Brad wouldn't share his blood with me. He'd share every other fluid, but that's where he drew the line. If I wanted to really take the next step in my training and career, I'd have to start drinking blood. You don't develop a taste for it like the horror movies say. You feel it join with your blood and everything amplifies. Good vibes only. You're on a cloud. The ecstasy wears off, but the energy remains. Bigger lifts, better ideas at work, more of that *joie de vivre*. That's how you get hooked. Not any cannibal pleasure. Like, who really loves the act of shooting heroin?

I breathe, holding this crazy bow that looks like an Affliction t-shirt that's been 3D printed to make a weapon for the guy who stole Tiger King's zoo. The Blues made it look so easy, their feet planted into the earth and their bodies perfectly still, braced yet relaxed, as they shot their arrows straight through the hearts of the targets. They didn't seem proud of their work; it was routine. That was what mastery looked like.

"What are you aiming for?" Doctor asks.

"I have to call it? What is this, Eight-Ball?" Laugh off the

48

nerves. Clearly screaming didn't settle them enough. Starstruck doesn't begin to cover it. That was for Justin Timberlake. Tom Hardy. Ryan Gosling. They may give butterflies in the stomach, but not the shiver down the spine or the heat coursing through my body. His energy is as contagious as a virus.

"That's a tough shot," he says. "You must be right on target to make that pay off. Do you have that level of focus?"

"Wait? What am I aiming for?" Laugh again. Maybe if you keep laughing, he'll think you made a joke. One that started the whole world crying. He smiles. Not like he thinks it's funny, but that it's OK, that he knows where I am.

"If you aim for the head, you must be sure you hit it, or your attacker will keep charging. It's a small target, so your odds of missing are high."

OK, we are talking about a battle. With those clowns who showed up last night? Maybe defending the farm was unrelated to the epic showdown of right and wrong Doctor discussed this morning. No Hell would send some semi-literate drunks in a pickup truck to bring about the end of days.

"The heart then. Like actual vampires," I say.

"Yes. Now, remember, you likely won't hit it. That is still a small target, especially when the body is moving. But, if you aim for the heart, you could very well hit a spleen, kidney, liver, stomach, or just cause massive bleeding. He'll lose his energy."

"The blood is the life."

"Very good. Now breathe."

He rests his head on my shoulder and the thirty or so people in matching white, gray, green, or blue athleisure attire fade away. His hands are on my hips, positioning them like Trevor sometimes did when correcting my form on a deadlift. His hands linger on my hips, then work their way up my back. He's gentle as he presses my left shoulder forward and pulls the right back and down, locking it into position.

"Now, pull back," he says.

My eye is locked on the target, vision in a tunnel like I'm looking through a scope. Concentrate. Focus. It's like lifting. Show your merit. Let your energy guide your arrow to the target. Silence. It's only me and the biggest ring on the torso.

Until the car engine and the sound of tires kicking up gravel jerks me out of my zen.

I keep focused on the target. If I can block out this distraction,

Bad Vibrations

I must really be filled with energy. Doctor's hands leave my hips. That must be my cue. I turn to see the police cruiser pulling into the compound.

Phoenix yanks the bow from my hands. He doesn't raise it to his shoulder, but the position at his side shows he will when he wants to.

Two men walk toward us. One's dressed as a sheriff's deputy in the tan uniform you only see in movies if you live in a city. Is that the same moron from last night? Not Royce, the one spouting all the malapropisms. He walks closer. It is. He's a cop. Maybe this would be war. The other looks like he was pulled from a drywall job.

"Aw, shit. Come on, Persephone," a woman in gray with tattoos says with a drawl, pulling a girl in matching gray by the hand. The older woman's tattoos aren't so much art, but dates. 2007 with "Kendall" in script. Likely the year of a child born. Maybe the teenager she drags right into the path to meet the two intruders.

"Hi Lori," the cop says. I didn't get the best view of him in the dark last night. He looks about forty, but the way these locals consume toxins, he could be twenty-six. The belt full of cuffs, billy clubs, guns, and walkie-talkies distract from the paunch like Man Spanx. He's wearing aviators like he must have heard cops are supposed to. His face is off-putting. Maybe it's the dour expression or the contemptuous dead-naming.

"That's not my name anymore and you know it," the tattooed woman says. Her teeth are yellow, not California bleach white like most of the others here.

"Apologies. Mind telling me how to address you these days?"

"Demeter."

"Demeter. That's right."

"What's he doing here?" Demeter nods at the man in the paint-splattered denim.

"Demeter, your husband wants to see his daughter."

"She's right here, Billy. Persephone never looked better, did she? No help from you." Demeter raises the teenager's hand. The girl stares at the ground. She's the youngest person here. So quiet. Aren't kids supposed to want all the attention?

"I just want to talk to her, Lori," Bill says. He's got that rugged handsomeness vibe going. Simple. Man who likes a beer after a long day working with his hands and a wife and kid to come home to. No great ambition. Probably shoots pool and builds things in

50

the garage. Lives day to day. It would be easier than wanting and striving.

"What do you want to say to her?" Demeter shouts. Persephone is by her side, expressionless like a disaffected teen, too cool to care. But that's usually an act. Persephone seems like she legit doesn't care at all. Push me where you want, keep grabbing my hand and shaking it at my dad, it doesn't matter. No fucks to give. It's either super cool or really sad. "Say you're sorry about the hole you punched in the wall? About trashing her room when she didn't clean it to your satisfaction?"

"I quit the booze two months ago and you know it." He's turning red.

"Oh, that's convenient. As soon as we leave, when no one can vouch for you."

"Lor-Demeter, I can attest that we've not picked Bill up recently. He hasn't been in the bars. He's a new man. You leaving made him see the light."

"Bullshit!" Demeter shouts.

"Deputy, you've upset my patient," Doctor says, stepping toward the mother and daughter. "If you have no official business, I'm going to have to ask you to take Mr. Bill here and leave the ranch."

"You twisted freak," Bill says. "You can't abduct my daughter into a cult! She's fourteen years old! You got someone drinking her blood, that's assault on a minor."

"Deputy, it's time for you to leave before this man drains all the energy out of my patients," Doctor says.

"Yeah, get the fuck out," Shane yells.

"You've got no right to come here and make accusations," Demeter says. "We're doing better here than we ever did out there. We found our wellness. All that shit trying to kill us, you can't live with us finding a way out."

"Now, everyone calm down. This town is big enough for all of us. But you folks gotta stay here and leave our folk to themselves. So, Demeter, hon, let's go on back with your husband now."

"Going back with him and his toxins is a death sentence!" Demeter says. Persephone continues to stare at her white Keds. "He's trying to kill us with his lifestyle. Who do you think you're protecting, Wade, sending us back with him?"

"I'm not trying to kill you, Lori, I'm trying to save my daughter from this insanity."

Bad Vibrations

"I'd say you are trying to kill us," Doctor says. "Your toxic attitude and way of life—the drinking, the processed food, the rage—kills more people every year than guns, terrorism, fire, and everything else you pretend is a big deal. On the whole, you make yourselves ripe for plagues. I take your presence in this sanctuary as a threat to our health. And I'm going to ask you again to leave."

"Families that stay together thrive together," the deputy says.

"Fuck yeah, they do," Medea shouts. "That's why we're all together here." She links her arm with Mentor's who links his with Andromeda's and it starts like a wave at a ballgame and Phoenix brings me into the chain.

"You're bringing in poison!"

"Toxic!"

The deputy turns to Bill.

"This ain't over, Lori. Kendall's coming home. I'll be back for her," Bill says.

"You'll never take her back to your death trap!"

"Death trap? You dumb bitch. How about when he tells you to drink the Kool-Aid?"

"Oh, that's original," Medea says.

The men turn and walk back to the cruiser. Everyone is shouting again like last night. Don't bring your death around here! You're cancer!

Everyone except Persephone.

Chapter 7

The group consultation feels kinda like a VIP festival experience. At least how I'd envision one. If I didn't know better, I'd think we were about to get into some ayahuasca. We're in Doctor's house, the ramshackle home with rusted siding for fronting and backing the drunk former owner let decay. According to Siren, an exterior paint job was on the docket. The interior renovations were first. For good reason. This consultation would have felt more like a seance if the inside matched the outside. We've only seen the living room; what lies beyond in this shotgun shack is a mystery. Maybe the walls are also painted a fresh white only interrupted by framed paintings of Doctor looking all kinds of saintly—fan art, as we're told, from the many talented people he has saved—and maybe the floors aren't yet refinished and mostly covered with white shag carpet.

A Himalayan salt lamp provides just enough light to see Faylor, Shane, Miami, and Doctor lounging in their hypo-allergenic palm thread beanbag chairs. The way you sink into them, it's almost like getting a hug, a security blanket that soothes and calms after all the surging heartbeats outside.

Faylor seemed most shaken by the invaders. Andromeda reassured her that the group consultation and the soft light of the lamp and the warm embrace of the beanbags were exactly what was needed. She was right. I didn't know I was tense until the chair melted the tension away. The touch I needed since Brad left. I could drift to sleep in this chair, but I don't because Doctor is speaking.

The salt lamp in the center of our little circle illuminates his face like a flashlight under his chin.

"I know you all want your names. You want your gray clothes. You want to attain optimal wellness. You're not going to get there without looking inside. Miami, this is your third event with us. Your friends Medea and Mentor brought you to us. Our cause and way of life fills you with purpose. This is what you were meant for, to spread the word, ask the ones who have not attained such a state if they've heard the good news. That there is a better way of life that provides salvation from the damnation of chronic disease. Am I right?"

"Yes. I'm so fulfilled when I engage in the ritual! And I feel that I'm doing the most important work of my life when I spread the good word. I thought I was doing important work when I was massaging feet! But, I mean, no amount of fascial release could ever help my clients as much as a single blood ritual. If I can convert one person to this way of life, my life is worth living."

"We are so lucky to have a true believer like you with such commitment. We're honored to have you, Harmonia."

"Harmonia? It's beautiful! Thank you so much!"

"Don't thank me. You have the most difficult work of your life ahead of you."

"I'm ready for it."

Miami, now Harmonia, beams, sinking back into her beanbag. Doctor turns his gaze to Faylor.

"Faylor, your road has been difficult. You've been bullied, shamed, disowned, never feeling like you truly belong. You're searching for an identity that represents you, and that your peers accept. You've tried to be the best version of you, and that has led to nothing but rejection. We've become your family and we accept you for who you are now and for the person you strive to be."

Faylor chokes back a sob. "Yes. You've all welcomed me. You're the family I've chosen. You didn't have to take me in, but you did. While my real family threw me aside, never understanding and allowing me to be all the people I've been to get to this point. I've been so alone since my goth friends cut me off and struggled until finding you and the prescription. When I met this family, it gave me hope that I'd finally found my identity."

"We accept you and are honored to have you, Atlas. Let us help carry the weight of the world."

Altas sobs now. The salt lamp illuminates the tears from supporting the weight of the world apparently. A little melodramatic for someone who swaps friend groups with easy labels every few years. Okay, Valerie. Stop judging. Maybe there's more to the story. Yeah, and maybe there's less.

"Shane, you've embarked on an endless quest in the pursuit of optimal wellness. You've found my prescription beneficial to that pursuit. But I need to know it's not just another stop, another box to check on your biohacking adventure."

"Doctor, I swear I'm not just passing through. I'm in this for the long haul. So committed I wanted to pitch you on a collab. I got the Ehans supplement line, you know."

"No, I don't." Doctor's warm, bedside tone turns to that of the clinician who wants you out of his office so he can prescribe the next diabetic.

"They're all science-backed supplements. Top-of-the-line game changers. We can put the blood in capsules and revolutionize the nutraceutical industry."

"You want to market blood capsules?" Doctor asks.

"I think we'd have to go through some legal shit, but it's nothing my team can't handle."

"You want to take part of my prescription and sell it on your Instagram account?" Doctor stares at Shane with eyes that can pierce your soul even in the dim lighting.

"Yeah. It would really get your message to the masses." He doesn't sound so sure of himself under Doctor's stare. It's like disappointing Dad.

"My prescription is a holistic approach. You can't just supplement blood and expect it to give you the energy you'd earn if you were following my prescription as written. The blood is the life, not a fad. It's not colloidal silver. It's blood. We're fighting for our health and that of as many people who will join us."

"Okay okay, got it. We'll table it. But I hope you see my commitment. I don't just offer to go into business with everyone."

"Yes, I see your commitment. To yourself, to your brand. You are Shane."

"That's cool. It's good to be Shane." He leans back in his beanbag. What are the nodes sending back to the dashboard? Did his heart even race when Doctor addressed him?

"Valerie." Doctor looks at me. If I were wearing the nodes, they'd be convinced I'd just done a max deadlift. "You've come to us frustrated. You're not reaching your goals. You've set some lofty ones. Make director at the agency, win your weight class in a powerlifting meet. But it's not working. You've been following the prescription and you're feeling physically better, but you're not getting that much stronger, are you?"

"No."

"You're not really training all that hard, are you? You're at the gym a lot, but you're skipping pieces you don't want to do."

"Yes."

"And you're no closer to Director of—what is it? Account services?—are you?"

"No."

"Because you're not putting the above-and-beyond effort in, are you? You're not selling clients new services, are you?"

"No."

"But you thought, if I follow this prescription, I'll achieve my goals."

"Yes."

"And it hasn't worked. And you know why."

"No, I don't." My heart is pounding. His eyes don't blink as they stare into mine. Deeper than my eyes. Into my soul.

"Yes, you do. But you just can't admit it because you hoped when you achieved them, you'd be happy. And you'll never achieve them. Can you tell me why?"

A lump forms in my throat. Huge and bulbous, it's choking me. The tears are coming, welling in my eyes. He wants me to say it. What do I say? What are the words? He's a human polygraph.

"I don't know." It comes out more desperate and less frustrated. Is that what I was feeling? Desperation for help?

"Because you don't want those things," Doctor says. "They're arbitrary symbols of achievement. They mean nothing to you. Your goals mean nothing to you."

A sob escapes. Then another. It doesn't matter who sees anymore. The words are all that matter. More than words. Truth. It breaks me.

"You told yourself when you got those things, you'd be happy. There was something missing and you thought those achievements would fill it. They won't because you don't want them."

"No, I don't! I don't want any of it! I don't even want to be an account manager; I definitely don't want to be in charge of them. I hate lifting. I just missed the competition I had in high school. But I hate it. I dread going to the gym. I hate my job and the stupid clients and their stupid problems and when they complain and complain about details that don't matter. The world is killing us, people are dying, and everyone else had a year of their lives taken away. And I have to tell them I care about the button colors on their stupid website? I hate it!"

"Valerie, you're here because deep down you've always known that. Your goals were never going to make you happy. And that's all you really want. You want to be happy."

"Yes. That's all I've ever wanted." The tears roll down my face. The lump starts to clear. It's a release.

"That's all that matters. Be well. Be happy. You've made a smart decision. You're in the right place, following the right prescription. We're honored to have you, Elpis."

"Elpis?"

"Elpis. Hope. Even though it's been misdirected, may you never run out of it."

Elpis. It's not as cute as Harmonia, and I'll probably have to explain it. But it's a lot better than Valerie and all the shit that came with her.

Chapter 8

Back in the barn, the four of us aren't outsiders anymore. We're still at the white table, but we're not tourists. We've been reborn into, like Atlas says, the family we've chosen. The Blues must be phlebotomists. Phlebotomist! What a fun word! What makes a word so fun? Why do we find certain combinations of words entertaining? Kumquat. Obliterate. Obfuscate. Words! What fun! It's like my mind is liberated for the first time in who knows how long. Years? Decades? All the noise and the static and the constant striving. And now? Oblong! Ragamuffin! Malarkey! Defenestration!

The blue phlebotomists phlebotomize us. Well, they swab our arms with alcohol and tie a cute, little tourniquet made of some sort of fuzzy, white fabric, then plunge the needle into the vein.

"Doctor is very impressed with you," Andromeda says as she swabs a wet cotton pad on my inner elbow where the good veins are.

"I've been living a lie for years. I'm more impressed with him for being the first to ever call me out on it."

"He sees potential in you."

"I sobbed like a baby in there. He tore down my illusions and it broke me. Nowhere to go but up. Hey, I guess that is potential."

"No, he sees it in you like he did in me. I resisted until he made it impossible for me to resist anymore. By resisting him, I was resisting myself."

"What happened?" Am I still resisting? Trevor used to say the same thing, that I was resisting all his advice. And Brad . . . what did he say? That I pushed him to the side to focus on me? That my goals were more important than him? Was that resisting? Is it yet another pattern this group has uncovered that I need to break?

"I went to one of Doctor's yoga retreats. I had a hot studio. Bikram," she whispers. "The guru was my hero. His practice changed my path in life. Then we find out he was a rapist and stole the practice from *his* guru. So, fuck him, right? I heard about Doctor's Yoga and thought I could explore all the options to rebrand my studio. I didn't think I could experience again what I felt that first time at Bikram." She whispers 'Bikram' again like the name will summon him here to turn the barn into a rapey sweat lodge. "Whatever I felt about the practice, Doctor felt about me. He kept asking me to dinner with him at his home. I kept refusing. He wasn't really my type. My ex was in a band, I liked riding on the back of his Harley. Finally I agreed to eat with Doctor if he agreed to stop asking. I canceled with my ex. He had invited me over to try and reconcile. While I was with Doctor, some drug addicts broke into my ex's house, thinking it was a dealer's. My ex fought them off, but the junkies stabbed him 34 times. If I'd been there, I'd be dead too. Doctor saved my life. I stopped resisting. Then he saved me again when I got sick. I was fucking meant for this. For him and his cause. Don't resist him. He'll save your life."

The blood leaving my body through the tube lightens me, like the last of the toxic thoughts have finally departed. As sacred as the ritual is and as euphoric as I feel, it all looks so clinical. It's science. No hokum. The blood is the life. How can anyone refute the prescription?

Andromeda leaves me with that tube in my arm, my blood seeping into a bag. Shane's tube mingles with the rest of his wires.

"Imagining how many capsules you can fill with that bag?" Atlas asks.

"Doctor will come around when he sees the dough we can make. I know angel investors. I can make it happen."

Before he can say anything else, I resume staring at my bag. So plentiful. Life in abundance. So much to share! If only the rest of the world could see us now. Thirty of the healthiest people around, on a perpetual quest for more and more wellness.

Andromeda removes the needle from my arm. She hands me some gauze and instructs me to apply pressure. She seals my blood bag and leaves it on the table to tend to Shane.

"I vant to drink your blood." Who knew Doctor could do a perfect Dracula?

"I didn't realize we joked about the whole vampire thing."

"Elpis, their pejoratives mean less if we use them in jest." Doctor smiles. He presses gauze into his arm just like I do.

"Who is drinking your blood?"

"Well, you. If you want it."

"Really? I'm just a White. Am I ready for it?"

"Elpis, you are worthy of happiness and fulfillment. It's why you're here. Don't you forget it." Doctor walks back to his table where he waits for the Blues to remove the tubes from the rest of the patients. The rest except Persephone. She's sitting next to her mom in her gray outfit. But no tube in her arm and no gauze. Her forearms rest on the table and she stares down at them. Maybe she's on her period. You can't give blood when you're already losing it. Was that in the prescription?

"Giving my blood, knowing that I'm giving life to my family—it's such a rush! I know it's like psychosomatic, but I already feel higher energy and vibrations from my blood leaving my veins, about to go into someone else's," Harmonia says. Her skin is as white as her crop top, but her smile is broad, authentic, in harmony with everything around her. The clean barn, its plywood floor still unfinished, the wooden beams looking like abstract art in the high, vaulted ceiling, the soft orange light of the setting sun glowing through the rows of small windows along each side, tables full of smiling, healthy people with faces exposed—harmony.

"Ever done a leeching?" Shane asks.

Harmonia shakes her head.

"Bro, the barber surgeons in the Middle Ages used that as treatment. They'd just cover a patient in leeches and draw out the toxins. They didn't call them toxins then, but it's all the same. After I got bitten by that tick on my survival school wilderness retreat, I went to a leech clinic in San Bernardino. That shit worked. Blew my mind."

"You willingly underwent medieval medical treatment?" Atlas asks with that tone reserved only for Shane.

"Medicine is cyclical. Ancient Chinese came back, didn't it? Medieval barber surgeons are next. Just open your mind."

Andromeda slides a shot glass onto the table in front of me. The dark red inside makes Doctor's etched cross logo pop.

"I swear people got into this because of how glamorous it looks in the shot glass," Shane says. "If the blood was served in a single-use Dixie cup, it wouldn't have looked as good on Instagram." Even Atlas has no response to that.

A sharp whistle brings attention to Doctor's table at the front of the barn right below the podium where he addressed us earlier. He's one of us now, on our level, holding a shot glass of blood. My blood?

"Family, we come together tonight to bring a day of life prescription to an end. The blood will infuse you with the high vibrational energy for a restorative sleep and the other energy-infusing activities you get up to in your cabins."

Shane raises his eyebrows at Harmonia. Fifty years ago, her smile would have been called sheepish.

"Let us raise our glasses," Doctor says. Thirty arms are in the air. "Thank you, family, for this blood we are about to receive. To the life!"

"To the life," we repeat. And down the hatch. Only regret? Doctor's blood is sipping blood. Top shelf. It's not some rotgut swill that needs to be fought down in a single gulp. But maybe that's why the lightness hits me so quickly. It rushes over me. A tingling that starts in my chest and vibrates all the way down to my toes. Did the room just become brighter? The euphoria of a new personal record in a lift at the gym. Only without doing the work.

"Damn, that hits the spot," Shane says, beaming, his white teeth sparkling. "Best I've felt since my ketamine journey. I never thought I'd feel as good as after my injection at the ketamine day spa out in L.A.—I even posted that, in those words! And, damn, this is just as good. Without the drugs."

"We need to tell the world about this," Harmonia says. "They need to know. Unlock their potential. Can you imagine the world if everyone just experienced what we're feeling now? Even just once."

"What if Putin tried the blood?" Atlas says.

"Oh my Doctor. If everyone tried it, there would be no wars!" Harmonia says.

"Seriously, Doctor is losing so much money not selling this. You could charge street drug rates per capsule and they'd still buy it. I can make it happen. I've just gotta make him see."

"Shh." Harmonia nudges Shane as Andromeda approaches the table and clears the shot glasses off the table into a wicker basket.

"Doctor has you scheduled for your one-on-one consultation right after we're done here," she says.

"How about me?" Atlas asks.

"Tomorrow morning."

Bad Vibrations

"Me?" Shane asks.

"Tomorrow afternoon."

"Where do I go?"

"You can just follow me," she says. "Bring your blood."

The other Whites follow us out with their eyes. Envy? Curiosity? It's hard to decipher their expressions. Ninety percent of communication may be non-verbal, but words are a lot more efficient.

Andromeda leads me out of the barn with her curves that should be in an old painting, dancing naked under a tree. Last night's unwelcome visitors clouded the galaxies with their smoke and exhaust and all-around bad vibes, but tonight the stars are glowing, radiating energy like me. Andromeda opens the door to the shotgun shack and feels through the darkness until a salt lamp illuminates the room enough to make my way to the beanbags.

"Doctor will be in shortly," she says. "Do not resist. He knows how to treat each patient."

She leaves me in a beanbag chair. It's more comfortable than any other doctor's waiting room. Hopefully after this treatment, I'll never need to go back to those fluorescent lights and probes and latex gloves. The blood will be my vaccine from now on.

The door creaks open, letting the light from the stars leak in.

"Elpis, how are you feeling?" Doctor asks.

"Like I'm closer to the heavens than I have ever been!"

"Good! That's what I want in my patients. Stay right under that Icarus level, take us to the limits of humanity. Did you enjoy my blood?"

"Yes! I wanted to tell you that taking a shot doesn't do it justice. You've got sipping blood. It should be in a chalice."

He laughs. "We all have sipping blood here. So many nutrients and so much energy."

"A capsule would really sell it short."

"Exactly. You are perceptive. Here, follow me." He offers his hand and I let him pull me up from the beanbag. He keeps it in his grasp as he leads me through the living room, through a dark room that appears to be a kitchen, and into the bedroom at the end of the home. He flicks on another salt lamp, revealing a similar aesthetic as the living room. White walls, only interrupted by abstract paintings and blackout curtains over the windows.

Doctor pats the lush, king-sized bed that takes up most of the room. "Come. Sit with me. We're on the same plane, you and I." Sitting on the bed, I can tell the sheets that appeared peach colored in the salt lamp light are bright white. Whose job is it to wash all the bedding? A washboard is the fastest way to get the toned arms you strive for, Doctor once said in his body transformation YouTube series. Hmm, mental note to look for the lady with the best arms and ask to help.

Doctor is just inches from me on the soft bed, but it's like he's all over the room, surrounding me.

"How has your time been here? Aside from the invaders, of course."

"OMG, I forgot about them! That's how transformative this time here has been. I feel . . . I feel light. Not like I did a cut or anything, but like I'm floating. It doesn't seem real. Is that the energy? I thought I knew what it was like, following the protocol on my own, but it's nothing like this."

"Have you performed an energy exchange with a partner yet?" He's looking into my eyes like there's no one else on Earth. What I think he wants to hear doesn't matter. He'll know the truth.

"Not really."

"What happened?"

"Medea tried to put me with Mentor, but we got interrupted by the . . . invaders. He isn't really my type anyway. I wasn't feeling any energy from him."

Doctor strokes my jaw, his fingers gentle, sending tingles through my body, more energy from that light touch than Mentor's or Phoenix's. "You have a prescription that needs to be filled." He runs his fingers up my thigh. We're gazing into each other's eyes and his hand works its way up my side until it gently cups my right boob.

"Wow. So much energy in these," he says.

"They keep me out of the 55kg weight class."

"But they store so much high vibrations." Gently, he massages both boobs. "This is where women store energy, the energy that feeds life. The only substance more pure than the blood is stored in the breasts."

"Have you drank it?" How did I get those words out with all the blood leaving my head? "Recently, I mean."

"No," he says, gazing into my eyes as he works his hand under my sports bra. "But I hope to do so eventually. For now, I do the closest thing." He pulls down the sports bra and leans in, sucking on my nipple like an infant feeding, like life is pouring out of me and infusing him with energy. Deep breaths. Is this really happening? To me? Like being picked out of a packed show for a backstage pass. Doctor. 600K YouTube followers. Another 350K on Instagram before they shut his account down. The one who will lead us from destruction.

And I haven't bathed today.

"So much energy," Doctor says, lifting his head back up to mine. "You need your fill." He slides his hand between my legs.

"Do you have a bathroom?" I don't mean to jump back, like I'm saying no. Don't resist. That's what Andromeda said. And I'm not. But how can I relax and be in a state to receive energy if I'm worried about being a sweaty mess?

"Right off the kitchen," he says.

Pulling the sports bra back up, I stumble off the bed. "I'll be right back. And so ready for you to administer my energy vaccine." Damn. Brad said I needed to work on my dirty talk.

Fumbling in the dark kitchen, I find a door and push it open. It's my lucky day; the bathroom, not a closet. I feel around the wall until my hand hits a switch. The darkness prevails. Yes, I can't quote it like Harmonia, but Doctor did have a video about the energy-sapping properties of electrical wiring. Such a relief to see a leader who actually practices what he preaches. There's gotta be a salt lamp in here somewhere. Yes! Is it the energy that is keeping me so light and happy even when I've likely sliced my hand on the rough edge of the lamp. Maybe he'll suck it right from my finger and I can give him the freshest blood he's tasted, rich in the nutrients it loses as soon as it's exposed to air, as Doctor says. Flicking the switch on the base illuminates the room and the lack of cut on my hand. Oh well.

I look in the mirror over the sink, shake my head, stifle a laugh. What am I so worried about? I've never looked better. This is the glowing skin all those supplement ads promised. But I've certainly smelled better. I turn the faucet and splash cold water under my arms, add some of the soap from the bar on the sink.

The faucet back off, I'm in silence again. With one last look in the mirror, I take a deep breath and open the door. My heart beats twice with every step through the dark kitchen and—

BANG.

Part 2

"Everybody needs to believe in something. I believe I'll have another beer."
—Fear

Chapter 9

My neighborhood back in Pittsburgh has a fun game called fireworks or gunshots. It's almost always fireworks. But those are screams. Fireworks don't have screams. That was a gun. More screams. I take the last step back into the bedroom. Another bang. More screams.

"Those shots were just to get your attention. The next ones are for real." The voice is clear through the thin walls of the shack. It's calm, unfamiliar.

"Help! Doctor!" a woman screams.

"Ah! Somebody get me a doctor!" A different man's voice, but high-pitched, mocking, almost singing. Laughter.

"We're here on suspicion of narcotics and corruption of a minor. You surrender the minor, we lose all interest in the drugs," the first, calmer man says. Drugs? "Now, I won't think twice about watching this bitch's brains explode all over this mighty fine ranch of yours."

"Think that'd make the soil inorganic or non-GMO or some shit, Sheriff?" A familiar voice. Cruel. Hint of a slur like there's liquor on the breath. Royce.

Doctor peers out the window that I hadn't even noticed when I was the center of his world. His head is peeking behind the curtain on the right. I follow his lead on the left. The darkness obscures the faces, but the glint of the gun held to Andromeda's head reflects the light of the stars. So does the sheriff's badge on the man's chest and the machete in Royce's hand. Three others stand with them. No visible weapons, but that means nothing. It's dark. They could have switchblades in their sleeves, gun holsters above their ankles, bombs in their shoes. Act like you're armed and like everyone else is too. Shelter in place. Or it's mutually assured destruction.

Bad Vibrations

"I know you can hear me," the man with the sheriff's badge says. "Lori and Kendall out here now. You can drink your blood and do your sick vampire sex shit, but you cannot poison my town. I'm giving you til the count of five and her brainwashed cult brain will be exploding all over the ground."

"Why won't they come out?" I'm thinking out loud.

Doctor says nothing, just stares out the window. By his expression, you wouldn't think his wife had a gun to her head. Simmering, maybe. Like he just got told his squat wasn't deep enough when he knew it was. But like a huge man with a badge and a gun is about to blow his wife's head up like a Peep in a microwave? No.

"Five."

"Doctor! She's your wife!"

Still nothing.

"Four."

"They're serious!"

"Three."

"Doctor, please!"

"Two."

Please.

"One."

Silence. No shot rings out.

Instead, it's Royce. "Really? All you vampire assholes just gonna let a fine piece of ass die?"

"Maybe they think you're bluffing, Sheriff," a woman's voice says.

"You see how much your little cult cares about you?" The sheriff gets his face right in front of Andromeda's while keeping the gun to her head, contorting her. It would be uncomfortable for anyone less proficient at yoga. "You drank the Kool-Aid, didn't you? And here you thought that was just a figure of speech. Just a way we teased your little cult. No, you really drank it. You did. You drank the Kool-Aid."

"Doctor, there's still time! I'll go get them," I say.

He grabs me and holds me back before I can take a step toward the kitchen, toward the one door I've seen in his hovel. He's holding me like the sheriff holds Andromeda. Don't resist him, she'd said. He'll save your life.

"I don't want to waste the bullet." The sheriff shoves

68

Andromeda to Royce. The drunk maniac yanks her long hair, tossing her head back. He raises the machete. It's over so quickly. It's hard to see the blood in the dark, but it must be a lot because Andromeda doesn't move. Her limp body slips from Royce's arms, disappearing into the blackness of the ground.

Doctor is stone-faced. No tears, not even a choked sob. He lets me go. I stay where I am. He was right; out there is death. She was right; don't resist.

"See that, Sheriff, you don't even need a stake to the heart to take these vampires out," the woman says.

"Which of you vampire motherfuckers is next?" Royce shouts.

Another scream. A man's this time. Obscured in the darkness, the figure stumbles to the ground, a long, slender object protruding from his chest.

"Aw shit," the sheriff says.

"Bill. Bill, are you alright?" The female bends to her knee over the man on the ground. Bill. Persephone's father. He screams in pain.

"Aw shucks, Sheriff, we shoulda took their arrows when we came down here earlier." The deputy. The idiot.

"Deputy Wade, I know Bill may not agree now with an arrow in his gut, but I'm glad you didn't."

"Why's that, sir?" the woman asks.

"Well, it sure gives us a good right to do what we're doing, don't it? It shows we got a worthy opponent. Violent. Dangerous. Now, isn't that exactly why we want them out? These vampires here are acting just like we said they would. Hell, we been saying they're a danger from the day they arrived. We didn't know how right we were."

How can someone be so calm with a corpse in a pool of blood and a gut-shot, screaming man at his feet? Doctor looks just as stoic. Which one is more terrifying?

"You want I should get him back into town? He's bleeding like a *stuffed* pig."

I look around the room. Maybe I could crash through the tiny back window. Get as far away from this stupid man as I can. The way this weird shack is laid out in a sideways shotgun, the front door puts me right in the clearing only twenty feet farther from the invaders and twenty feet closer to my car than this big window. At least the small one puts me in the field where they may not see me running to God knows where.

"Yes, drop him at Dr. Roberts and get right on back here," the sheriff says.

"C'mon, Bill." The deputy extends his hand to the man groaning on the ground. Bill's not getting up. "OK, Bill. Now don't be mad at me. It's *fer* yer own good." The deputy kneels right behind Bill's head and loops his arms under the injured man's shoulders. He tries to stand but drops Bill back on the ground. Another scream. "Well, I'm sorry, Bill, but I warned you this wasn't gonna be real pleasant."

"Shari, give him a hand," the sheriff says.

Shari, the woman who finally steps into enough light to reveal a uniform that matches Deputy Wade's, slides her hands under Bill's shoulders and loops her arms under his and up to his chest, locking her hands. She takes a couple steps backward, then releases her hands and Bill crashes back to the ground.

"That's how you do it, Wade," she says.

Wade gives it another try, and Bill's wailing agony tells me how it's going while I turn to Doctor who is still staring out the window.

"Damn. You couldn't pick up a hooker with a desperate meth habit," Shari says.

With technique that coach Trevor would say is a slipped disc waiting to happen, Wade deadlifts Bill's torso from the ground and starts dragging him backward toward the road. Bill's white sneakers are the last thing to slip out of view.

"What's next, Sheriff? Looks like they don't care much for this one." Royce kicks Andromeda's corpse. He's not wrong. Why did Doctor pursue her like he did, save her life from the home invaders then the virus, only to let this new round of invaders murder her?

"No, it doesn't, does it, Royce?"

"No, sir."

"So much for their talk about being a family. That's what cults do. We'll see what happens when—"

An arrow lands in the ground, maybe a foot from the sheriff's foot.

"Just keep making bad decisions," the sheriff says.

"Sheriff, we got a problem," Wade yells from out of my view.

"What is it, Deputy?"

"One of them vampires shot an arrow into our tire."

"Well, that's a damn shame, ain't it," the sheriff says as he lights a cigarette. The man is a walking toxin.

"You want I should just leave him over here for now. He's looking a little *pecan*."

"Yes, Deputy. We're just going to have to make this a little quicker than I'd hoped." Another arrow hits the ground. "Now, Royce, if they don't knock off this nonsense, we're just gonna have to go to Plan B."

"I got that right here, Sheriff." Royce taps his foot on a white barrel with what looks like a nozzle attached. How did I miss that?

"How do you say that word again?"

"Glyphosate." Royce over-enunciates, real loud, making sure we all hear. Round-Up. Pesticide. Poison.

"That's it," the sheriff says. "We know all about you folks. We've seen you on the YouTubes. It's easier than sunlight on a real vampire. At least they don't advertise their Kryptonite. If it ain't organic, it's toxic. And toxic equals toxins and toxins equal death."

"Bunch of new age, hippie horseshit, if you ask me," Shari says.

"He's starving us out," I say.

Doctor still doesn't reply, just stares out the window. I stop talking. He already knows. He saves lives. He's a doctor. What do I know compared to him? Trust him. Don't resist. We're out there, firing arrows. Doctor has it under control. Royce hasn't sprayed our crops yet. Or has he? Where is he?

"Deputy Adkins," the sheriff says.

"Yes, sir?" Shari Adkins says.

"Let's get back to why we're here."

Shari pulls the pistol from her cop belt of tricks. She's got two hands on it like real cops, not gangstas in the movies. She knows what she's doing. Remember that. She approaches the barn and kicks in the door. An arrow flies into her thigh. She shuts the door and staggers from it.

"Shit!" she cries, not with tears, but with rage. She puts the gun back in her belt and yanks the arrow out of her leg, tossing it to the ground like it's a minor inconvenience.

"You alright there, Shari?" Wade asks.

"Yeah, I'm fine. Except these vampire freaks shot me with a fucking arrow!"

"Are our girls in there?" Royce's voice. He's not far away.

"They shot me before I could tell. But there's a lot of them in there, I can tell you that."

A tap on glass jolts me more than the flying arrows. It's coming from the back of the room, the wall abutting the fields of crops. Doctor jumps from his post at the window and hops over the bed to the other side. He flings back the curtain and the window creaks open.

"A lot of them, huh?" the sheriff is saying.

"Yeah, looks like at least twenty vampires."

"Where's Persephone?" Doctor says in little more than a whisper.

"With Phoenix. Demeter, too. Persephone wasn't feeling well, so they took her to the cabin. Phoenix is standing guard," a woman whispers.

"What about everyone else?"

"Everyone is still in the barn."

Doctor walks back to the window, around the bed this time. Siren is right behind him with a bow in her hand, a quiver of arrows on her back. Doctor's holding a bow as well. You'd need her agility to get through the window with all those weapons.

"I left to go shoot out the tire."

"Good thinking," Doctor says.

"Let's take a different tact," the sheriff says in that laconic drawl. "More diplomatic." He knocks on the barn door. "Now, we don't want more bloodshed. Just give us Kendall and Lori and we'll be on our merry way. They're in there, aren't they?"

Quiet. At least from the shack. The sheriff must hear something because he says, "Now, there's no need for that language. We're here on behalf of a man who just wants his family back."

The sheriff and his deputies flank the door, hands on their guns, ready to draw. Where's Royce?

"Nazis? No, we're not Nazis. Just local law enforcement. And with the power vested in me by this community, I'm giving you one last chance. Send out Lori and Kendall."

Doctor and Siren are back at the window, watching the barn.

"They're telling the truth," Siren mutters. "Leave them alone."

"Well, deputies, I think that even with all that profanity, they're telling the truth. Our girls aren't in there."

"I second that," Shari says. She shoves her gun back into her belt and detaches something else. She pulls it over her head. Goggles. Huh?

"Ditto," Wade says.

"I guess we'll just be moving on to the next bunker," the sheriff says.

They don't move.

"I don't like this," Siren says.

Doctor raises his compound bow, takes a step toward the kitchen, toward the front door. Siren follows. She beckons me. The intruders outside can't hear the ancient floor creaking, but we creep through the home like we're the ones breaking and entering until we reach the living room.

Only one of us is unarmed. The corner, low on the floor, is a good place for me. Siren pulls two arrows out of her quiver. She hands one to Doctor. He flings open the front door as Royce walks toward the barn. His arm is raised. The moonlight reflects off the canister in his hand. Hairspray? Anything aerosol is banned in Doctor's Prescription. Talk about free radicals! But that's a long, slow death of cancer years down the line, not the quick brutality that marked the end of Andromeda. He stops at the barn door. Doctor is outside, his bow pulled back, taking his time, breathing, concentrating, aiming at the ample gut of the leader of these intruders. Royce nods.

Doctor snaps the back of the bow as Shari kicks the door open again. Royce raises the canister and lobs it into the barn. Screams. Doctor's arrow bounces off the sheriff's back. Shari, goggles on and gun drawn again, unleashes a torrent of bullets in the barn. I sink to the floor but blocking my view of the attack amplifies its sounds. Without anything to look at, I picture the mayhem in the barn. My terrified family, running from the bullets, yet inevitably falling to the ground in agony, clutching the bleeding holes in their bodies. Their lives gushing out of them onto their matching uniforms as they flop and flail and scream on the floor of the barn.

The sheriff's posse backs away from the barn, arrows ricocheting off their chests and backs, others hitting the ground next to them. The sheriff pulls his gun from his holster. Doctor and Siren rush back inside the house and shut the door. The arrows keep flying. The screams are dying down. There was comfort in the screams. Life, even if they were just hanging on. Now they're softer, fewer. Another arrow bounces off Shari's chest.

"If y'all haven't figured out we're wearing Kevlar vests, you must be so dumb you'd die for those two bitches," Shari says. "You give us the girls, we leave you alone."

"Can't we just give them up?"

"Shut up, Elpis," Siren says.

"But they'll kill us."

"Then why are you here? Did you miss every word Doctor said? It's war. This is the war. I guess it was all good for you when it was yoga and blood and sex, but this is what we've been training for."

"I, I didn't think it was a real war."

"Of course it's a real war," Doctor says. "I'm a doctor. I don't speak in metaphors. These are the four horsemen of the apocalypse. We will be the last ones standing. We are strong in body and mind. They may bring destruction, but we bring rebirth." Doctor grabs another arrow from Siren's quiver.

"I bet you're wondering what's going on in the barn, why you can't hear your fellow vampires screaming anymore. Well, that's because they're all dead. Shari's a hell of a shot. You get a lot of target practice when you're in the sheriff's department. And that's what you gotta remember here. You're not in all that great standing with the law, now are you, doctor? So I'd recommend again, give up the girls."

Doctor's face doesn't change. Not in great standing with the law? What does that mean? If this is the local law, who could possibly be in good standing?

"Now, my deputy tells me you had no more than twenty congregants here."

"That's how I counted 'em, yessir," Wade says.

"So what say we go door to door?" the sheriff says.

"Like Jehovah's Witnesses." Shari pushes the goggles up to her forehead.

"Right. Until we find ourselves those two. Royce, can I get a witness?"

"Be my honor." Royce picks up his machete from the ground where he must have dropped it after what appeared to be tear-gassing my new family. He walks from the barn toward the end of the compound where the man with the arrow in his chest is probably dying or at least in severe pain. Maybe Bill is wondering how his life came to this. How he just went to this ranch to find something he thought he needed so bad. And now he's sheltering in place, waiting for death to come.

Machetes, or maybe even a bullet for the ones the sheriff deems worthy. Asshole.

It wasn't apparent until Royce's ominous walk that the cabins are arranged in a hierarchy. Mine across from Atlas and Shane's are the closest to the entrance. Where the pawns line up. Most of the grays occupy the next six cabins—three on each side—then two for the greens. Doctor's shack is in the prime location right across from the barn, while another cabin—must be where the other two Blues live—is right beside the barn. Like a sacrificial queen. But Royce isn't there yet, he's sauntering, machete at his side, toward my cabin. He's walking with a swagger like he learned his gait from Michael Myers. Please, please, please no one be in there. Harmonia, Mentor, Medea, please have run to the fields.

Royce is at the door. It's too dark to see what he's doing. Is he knocking? The blade glimmers in the moonlight.

"What the fuck?" Royce jumps back from the door, machete still in hand. "Fuck!"

"What's going on over there, Royce?" The sheriff asks. Does that man register a pulse?

"Vampire fuck threw a power tool at me!"

"A power tool?"

"It's not a power tool?" Royce asks. Who is he talking to? "A pulsating deep tissue what?"

Shane. Of anyone to have survived.

"Shut the fuck up! Is Kendall in there?" Royce isn't quite shouting, but he doesn't have the command of the sheriff's quiet calm. He's got the loose-cannon role down. If Shane's this calm arguing semantics maybe his fear training was legit. Or, he's thinking like me. Royce is a madman who I want as far away from me as possible, but the man who can maintain a zone 1 heart rate while sentencing an innocent woman to death . . . those are the men who start wars.

"Yeah, I will come see for myself." Royce disappears into the cabin. Unless Persephone flattened herself like Bugs Bunny and is hiding under the weighted blanket, there's nothing more to see inside the tiny, one-room cabin than from the doorway. A light shines from the cabin. Royce emerges.

"She's not in here."

"Who is in there?" Shari asks.

"Some asshole with wires all over his chest and a hippie girl. She's kinda hot. Shame she drinks blood."

"Bring them out, Royce."

"Now, Siren," Doctor says.

I must have missed a cache of weapons in the darkness of the living room because Siren has a Super Soaker at her side. You can see it's neon and obviously a squirt gun as she runs from the door of the cabin. She pulls the trigger. A dark spot grows on the back of the sheriff's tan shirt. Blood. The moron deputy turns toward her just in time to take some AB negative in the face. He lets out a howl like a disappointed dog and immediately rubs his hands over his eyes, which of course, rubs more blood in them.

Shari's reaction is also canine, but more like a junkyard dog, ready to pounce when she sees the source of the attack. She barrels toward Siren, undeterred by the bloodstream from the water gun, and knocks the erstwhile influencer to the ground. She rips the Super Soaker from Siren's hands. She fooled a lot of people, convincing them her resistance band and tiny dumbbell workouts made you strong. If you were really working the posterior chain like her reels claimed, you'd be a lot harder to knock down.

Shari's got her pinned on her back. She straddles Siren, sitting on her toned abs and unloads the Super Soaker point blank into her face. It's hard to watch the blood fill her nose. She gasps for breath and it fills her mouth and it's like she's drowning in blood. Siren thrashes her arms and legs.

Doctor jumps out the door and pulls back the bow. The arrow lodges in Shari's shoulder. Her scream is like a dog, too. She leaps off Siren, who immediately turns her head and coughs up blood. Shari yanks the arrow out of her deltoid and throws it at Doctor. It misses. He leaps back into the cabin, leaving Siren outside writhing, choking on blood.

"Death. Do you see this, Elpis? Evil. The evil sickness of the world has never been more malignant and aggressive. We can't go back to that world. Never." Doctor is pacing in the tiny space by the door.

"What about Siren?"

"Everyone we lose is a tragedy, Elpis. Terrible tragedy. But her life still matters—"

Where he was going with that will have to remain a mystery; the sheriff is speaking.

"Alright, Doctor Howell. It's time to give up. You know what you've done is wrong. You've moved into our community and took advantage of a vulnerable farmer to take his property. He's in the bars now, no livelihood to speak of. You've imposed your warped way of life on our town and corrupted our youth." He steps on

Siren's chest. She gurgles. He shifts his weight onto her ribs. "We want the girl back. She should be with her father. Now, I wouldn't advise wasting any more of my time."

"You'll never take her back," Doctor shouts. "My warped lifestyle? Your sick way of living doesn't support the life that girl deserves."

"OK then," the sheriff says. He lifts his foot from Siren's chest and she starts to sit up. His foot collides with her face with such force that she's knocked back on the ground. The sheriff takes a step toward her. Her head lolls on the ground. The sheriff stomps his foot into her forehead. Since she's already soaked like a telekinetic prom queen, it's hard to tell if there's any new blood. The crunching sound makes me look away.

"Oh, stop crying, you baby," Shari says. Who is she talking to? Oh. Harmonia and Shane walk slowly, the end of Royce's blade grazing their backs. "You all come here with your city privilege and just take what you want. Our land. Our children. Bitch, you deal with the consequences when we take it back."

Harmonia clings to Shane. They're moving closer to the bloody corpses on the ground with Royce's blade slicing the air at their backs. Shane's wires are dangling off him, tangled in his white tank top.

"He's wearing a wire! Sheriff, he's got a wire!" Deputy Wade shouts. He marches up to Shane, brandishing his service revolver. "Who are you working with? The Feds? This is our bust, boy. You're out of your jurisdiction."

"It's not that kind of wire, bro."

"It looks a Hell of a lot like a wire to me!"

"Yo, it's a wire, just not what you use them for."

"Then what's it for then?"

"Wade, it's like medical or something. Probably tests how much blood he's got flowing since he drank so much," Royce says. "Can't have him running out of blood now. What do you all say? It's the life, ain't it?"

"You're real close, bro. It's about getting optimal blood flow to pump to my muscles in training so I'm recovering while I'm training. Get it?"

"No," Royce says.

"No," Wade says.

"Fuck no," Shari says.

"So you don't lose blood flow ever! Man, it'll help you sustain machete swinging longer. I've got discount codes if you guys want. I can hook you up."

"The self will get you nowhere, Shane," Doctor says. "Elpis, we'll be taking decisive action. I'll need you to go light them on fire."

"What? Who? How?"

"All of them. With a Molotov cocktail. And I suspect your next questions will be when and where. When is as soon as they separate from Shane and Harmonia. Where is wherever they are."

"But how? How do you set someone on fire? I thought those were like for buildings."

"Yes, they are. But if the people are soaked in kerosene, they will immolate. This is your mission, Elpis. The future of humanity depends on it. You run to the shed on the farmland. You know where it is?"

"I saw it earlier today."

"Yes. It's too far to be visible at night. Go there. You'll find the kerosene for our lamps and the gasoline for our farming equipment. Take a lighter from one of the shelves. There are many. And light them on fire."

"I—I don't know if I can light a person on fire."

"Oh, Elpis. You will be amazed what you are capable of. It's who you are. You who have abandoned all artificial goals and pretense to find your purpose. This is it. It cannot be more important. You have it in you. We all do."

"Can't I just shoot them with an arrow?"

"We're a little too late for that. If we'd been poised for combat at our stations, it would have been a fine approach. We could have fended them off. But these cowards attacked at night. And now they're inside and we have to take drastic measures. You have to light them on fire."

Visualize it. Like coach Trevor used to tell me on my big lifts. My visualizations were always a lot of weight and someone else lifting it. The girl tossing my idea of WTF a Molotov cocktail is—a whiskey bottle with a flaming rag stuck out the top?—isn't Elpis, not even Valerie. Are the two really different? Neither one can immolate people, not even her enemies. But both need to get out of here.

Screams outside. Not terror. Rage. "Get the fuck off me! Bitch!"

"How do I get to the shed?"

"Hey. Sheriff!" Shari's voice drowns out my question and the profanity outside. "Look what I found."

Shari pushes Demeter out of the cabin, gun pressed into her back. Wade rushes over.

Demeter keeps screaming. "Stupid fucking bitch! You're making a huge mistake!"

"No! You made a huge mistake, Lori." Bill, arrow stuck out of his gut, hobbles past my cabin. He coughs, spits, probably blood. It was just an hour ago we were all drinking it. To life. Now it's death.

"Bill, you shouldn't be trying to walk now," the sheriff says.

"It's my family." Bill wheezes. The arrow must have punctured a lung. Painful, but not instantly fatal. Doctor was right. Arrows aren't enough. Doctor is always right. Whatever he tells me to do will be right. At first, the diet seemed counterintuitive to lifting gains. It wasn't. He's been right all along. The diet, the yoga, the blood, the kill shots, the goals.

"You're not our family," Lori—Demeter—screams. "You were killing us!"

"I've got her," Wade says, holding Persephone by her wrist. Unlike her mother, she doesn't resist. She's a teenager only on the outside.

"Kendall, baby, it's time to go home," Bill says.

"We're not going anywhere." Lori stomps her foot into Shari's, freeing her from her captor's arms for a split second. That's all she needs. She pulls a knife from the high waistband of her yoga pants and slices at Wade's arm. He wails, and when Wade lets go of Persephone to grab his presumably bleeding forearm, Lori takes his place. She stands behind her daughter, one arm around her waist and the other, the one with the blade, at her neck.

"Lori, let her go. You don't want to do this. She's our daughter."

"She's not your daughter anymore. She's a woman. She makes her own decisions." Lori pulls Persephone tighter, shaking, the blade dangerously close to her neck. Persephone just stands there, limp.

"She's fourteen. And you and that doctor quack make all the decisions for her."

"Oh, you have no idea," Lori says with a derisive laugh. "She's the future. She carries in her the savior of our health. What she'll give to us will lead us to salvation. The perfect specimen, born with more energy than you could imagine, to show people like you what's possible."

"What are you talking about, Lori?"

"You're not fucking up another generation. You're not taking something with so much energy and wellness, something that powerful and turning it into shit with your evil life."

"Go now, Elpis," Doctor says. "While they're occupied. Take this." He rushes to the bed and reaches underneath, pulling out another off-brand Super Soaker.

"Blood?"

"Cayenne pepper and vinegar. Use it like mace. Go now. Out the back window where Siren came in."

The small dresser in the bedroom gives me a boost out the window. Crawling through is easy after tossing the water cannon out onto the ground. Seated on the sill, my feet dangle a couple inches from the ground. It's a soft landing in the grass. The supply shed is on the right, toward the crops, away from the shouting.

"Lori, please let her go. We'll get her help," Bill says. If I was still inside, I may not have been able to hear him.

"She's got everything she needs here."

"Who did this to her? Who did this to our little girl?" Bill chokes. It may not be the arrow, but the lump in his throat that's making Bill's voice nearly inaudible.

"No one did it to her. It's an honor. To be carrying the child from a man with more energy than anyone in the world."

And for a second time today, everything comes crashing down.

Don't resist, Andromeda had said. How many others did she advise? Did she say that to Persephone? It's not about the blood or the energy or even this war we're in. It's about what it's always about. How am I so stupid? It's about fucking young girls.

The shed is to the right; the woods to the left behind the barn. Sneaking through the trees can get me to my cabin and my keys and my car.

Shane and Miami—she is Miami, a thinking being capable of controlling her own destiny, not Harmonia, some cog in the movement's machine—have the same idea. With Royce and his machete closer to Lori and Kendall, his first two prisoners run past the barn and disappear into the black night woods. Wade pulls his gun and aims it at a forest.

"Let them go," the sheriff says. "They won't get far." Because of the darkness? Are they underestimating Shane because of his wires? Or is there something else lurking in the trees and bramble?

"Lori, let go of her." Bill, arrow in his chest, steps closer. "Put down the knife. She's your daughter."

"That's right, She's my daughter! I'm the one that took her from your toxic life. Drinking, shouting, whoring!"

"Hey, look, Lori!" Royce is back at the barn, waving his machete for attention. "Maybe this here'll change your mind." Royce opens the barn door. He disappears inside. No. No one needs to see what's inside. Like the refrigerated trucks lurking near the hospitals in NYC. You know what's in them. No need for a tour.

Royce does one better. Of course he does. Sick fuck. We all knew it from the moment he came into the diner. We must have just denied it. Like we denied what we all must have known about Doctor. In one hand he holds what appears to be a small, clear vial. In other, he drags a corpse in white. Faylor.

"Looky what I found!" He waves the vial over his head. "Motherfuckers all holier than thou about not drinking or smoking, but they've got ketamine in here."

"You called it, Sheriff!" Wade says, patting the sheriff on the back. "You said no way people get that happy from blood, had to be a drug mixed in there."

"I only know from my experience, Deputy," the sheriff says.

Ketamine? No, it can't be drugs. The blood can't be a lie too. But, what if? Be present, just like poor @Lululunges said. If you are on drugs, it's more important than ever. Focus. Be present.

Royce drags Faylor's body near Lori's cabin, delivering it like a cat takes a dead mouse to the door. Surprise!

"There's plenty more where that came from!"

Lori's shaking, but no more than she already had been. She's got the leverage, but she's not in control. None of us are.

"OK, Lori. Enough of this game," the sheriff says. "Look what your antics gone and done. I didn't wanna have to gas your friends, but seeing how you wouldn't leave and let our precious Kendall come home, well you left me no choice but to kill all these people."

"They're dead?" Lori's voice trembles. No more of that daytime talk show, you-stole-my-man rage.

"Yes," the sheriff says. "Now, why don't you put down the knife and we'll take you home?"

Lori laughs. "We are home."

She slashes the knife into Kendall's neck and blood gushes out.

Kendall's hands rush to the wound, but the blood just flows through her fingers, and she falls to the ground.

"No!" Bill leaps toward his daughter and trips, driving the arrow deeper into his chest. He stays there, impaled, the arrow now jutting out of his back as well as his front. The sheriff's gun is raised. He fires three shots. Lori hits the ground.

Go to the shed. Fuck the doctor. Fuck the prescription. A fireball will get you out of here.

"Bill's dead." Shari's kneeling beside him, holding his wrist.

"A whole family destroyed by a vampire cult." The sheriff removes his hat and holds it over his chest. "They'll keep doing this to more families if they're not stopped. How does a fourteen-year-old girl get pregnant with her mother right here?"

"Hey, Sheriff," Wade says. "You know I'm a bit of an authority on these folk. All the research I done on them on the YouTubes and all."

"What are you rambling about, Wade?" Shari asks.

"Well, these vampire folk talk a lot about energy and they say the doctor's got the most of anyone—"

"Lori said the father had the highest energy." The sheriff puts his hat back on his head, pulls his cigarettes out of his shirt pocket and lights another. "Ain't that a cult leader cliche? We're just gonna have to pay the doctor a visit. Make it impossible for him to go on raping our children."

"I saw him go into poor old Dennis Kirsh's house," Shari says.

"You want I should chop his cock off?" Royce asks.

"No, Royce. I'm thinking something slower. Make him have some real remorse right before the end. After all, he's the leader. He brought this plague into our town. He's responsible for all of it. And for everything that happens to his little vampire congregation here."

The sheriff's tone is so even, so reassuring. He has a bedside manner. Like a doctor, a good doctor. Like Doctor. There will be no appealing to his or his posse's human decency. They're under his spell.

They walk toward the shack. The time to flee is running out. Right to the supply shed and the flammables. Left to the woods and whatever lurks in there. Visualize it. You're throwing the flaming bottle. Like middle school softball. No, visualize something that went better. It's there. Someone better than me. One of the girls who knew how to throw. Someone with better velocity and aim. Someone who could know what a man on fire looked like, smelled like, screamed like and could throw an aerosol bomb with any semblance of competence.

They're out of my line of sight. It's now or never. Legs better still have it. Don't sprint without warming up, they'd say. You'll pull a hammy, they'd say. Muscle memory plants my left foot forward and explodes off the right in the back. I'm almost to the barn. Hamstrings are fine. Adrenaline coursing. A gunshot rings out.

"We'll get her later," the sheriff says.

Whichever one fired doesn't matter. None of it back there does. The woods are steps away. My pace slows, like the blackness of the woods is a wall.

They won't get far, the sheriff had said. If that's true, hopefully I'll have some company in the total darkness. Blind, I step forward, deeper into the black. A stick snaps beneath my foot. That's how they'll find me, crashing through the forest like Ray Charles and making just about as much noise too. Maybe they'll find me knocked unconscious in a bed of moss, having walked into a low hanging tree branch. Dead leaves crunch. It's not getting any less black. Running is not an option. Slow, deliberate steps are the only way forward, though they take me longer to escape my would-be captors. But they could also grab a flashlight and find me in an instant. Just walk forward, away from the light. Keep hands outstretched.

Shit! The tree bark is sharp. Move on. Keep walking. But to where? Town? The sheriff's town? Be the vampire girl asking for help to escape their elected official? The man who won a popularity contest to protect and serve them? Oh my god, that's what he's doing. Protecting them from us.

Don't think so far ahead. Like they say, stay in the moment. Be present. One step at a time. Live in the now. The black, prickly, crinkly, lonely now.

Chapter 10

Does it never rain here? Maybe the sheriff has such low expectations of our survival in these woods because they're part of some vortex that's immune from Pennsylvania weather systems. It wouldn't be the strangest thing I've experienced today. How else would you explain the brittle, dry leaves that crunch under my feet with every step? Maybe the trees are all dead. Standing dead. Zombie trees. That would explain the sticks on the ground. Right foot. Left foot. Right. Snap. Crackle. Fuck!

My big toe throbs. If it's broken . . . No! My body isn't fragile. Just stop for a moment. Let the pain run its course. Breathe.

The throbbing subsides. Time to move on. One quick look back. Yes, there is still the faintest light. I may not know where I'm going, but I sure know that I'm getting far away from where I've been. Here I go again.

Leaves crunch. A lot of them. Almost like the sound of running through them. But my feet are planted, unmoving. It's like a cacophony of leaves, a tornado coming toward me. Stay still. The tornado stops. Is that a whisper? The footsteps smashing through the brush have stopped. Where are they? They could be anywhere in the blackness. No sound. No movement. This place offers no shelter. It's time to go. Crunch.

Snap. Crunch. Snap, snap, snap! Each of my delicate steps is met with a flurry of noise. I stop. Silence. Right foot. Snap. Crunch, crunch, crunch.

Something collides with my shoulder and I'm on my back, the water gun falls out of my hand. Human? Yes. Arms are wrapped around my ribs and nothing is gnashing at my face, no talons clawing at my flesh. No time to scream. The hand fumbles and tries to find my mouth. Fingers between my lips. I bite down.

"Ow!" It's a man's voice.

I grab at him, feeling blindly through the air, coming away with nothing. Where is he? His hands are still holding me down, but the rest of him is out of reach. Finally something brushes against my waving hand. String. I pull on it. The sound of tearing skin. A finger slides into my mouth, quickly pulls out. Lesson learned. Something light lands on my chest. The string is in my hand.

As the hand slides back over my lips, before it can press down, I say, "Shane?"

"Who the fuck are you?"

"Valerie. Get your hands off my face."

"Elpis!" Miami must be approaching. The leaves crackle.

"How do I know that?" Shane asks. Now that he's figured out where my face is, he's moving his hands down to my neck, getting in strangling position.

"Why would anyone pretend to be me right now?"

"Why is anything like it is right now?" he asks.

"Are you guys trying to get to town?"

"We're waiting here for Doctor's orders," Miami says.

"Doctor's dead."

"No. He can't be," Miami says. "Doctor has too much energy."

"Maybe not yet. They may still be torturing him, but he'll be dead soon." The sticks and pine needles and whatever else covers the forest floor scrapes my legs, poking through the yoga pants, as I crawl to get up. The white fabric must be soaked in blood, all the energy collected throughout the day seeping out from the bramble and these sad shrubs. I stay on my knees, feeling around the prickly brush for the water gun that moron knocked out of my hands.

"They can't torture Doctor. He won't allow it. His energy is too great," Miami says.

Something sharp embeds itself into my palm. Odds are it's not a used hypodermic. I keep feeling around. "He doesn't have energy. None of us do." My hand touches plastic. Oh thank God. The smooth cylinder filled with pepper spray.

"Don't talk like that," Shane says. "We need solidarity right now. It's us versus them."

"You're right." The water bazooka is back at my side and my legs are out of the brambles. "It's the three of us versus them. I've got a water cannon filled with cayenne pepper. Or so Doctor says. What have you got?"

"We picked up some sticks out here," Shane says. "And I'm feeling like my heart rate's still down. I'll get us out of here."

"Why do you keep implying Doctor's lying?" Miami asks.

"Because he lies. About everything. Screaming during yoga doesn't detoxify you. There is no energy. The blood isn't the life. That's just a line from an old book like the haters say. It's ketamine that's making us all feel so euphoric after taking it."

"What's wrong with that? Psychedelic medicine is clinically proven to be the future of mental health treatment," Shane says. "Studies show."

"Sure, but I don't want to be drugged without my permission. It just gets our guard down so we can convince ourselves there's a method to all this weird shit, and it gets young girls to fuck old men."

"Sex is part of the prescription," Miami says.

"How about knocking up teenagers?"

"What are you talking about?"

"Persephone. Doctor got her pregnant. She's fourteen. He's like all the rest. Children of God. Manson. Nxium. Just an old man who wants to fuck young girls and brainwashes them to do it. And this is Waco."

"You just threw a lot of shit out there, bro." A glow in the dark, like a tiny star, but barely higher than eye level.

"Are you checking your heart rate?"

"My tension score," Shane says. "That'll tell me if I think you're lying."

"Why don't you just know if you think—never mind. What is your watch telling you?"

"That I'm fucking tense. We gotta move."

"And go where?" Good question, Miami.

"Get out of here."

"Do either of you have your phones?" I ask.

"No."

"No."

"Why didn't you grab them? You were in a cabin!"

"I wasn't in my cabin, bro. That's where my phone was."

"Mine was out of power," Miami says. "I forgot to turn off the Wi-Fi. I think it died searching for a network."

"Like us," I say. "So how do we get out of here?"

"Due north," Shane says.

"Which way is that?"

"We go toward the north star. Polaris. Works every time. Learned that in darkness training. It was mostly to enhance my other senses, but at that camp in the desert I took a lot of notice of the stars. And they helped me find my bearings better than my nose could. Mind blowing. You don't know what you can do til you do it. Didn't think I'd make it at first. But I did. And we will now. Just look up. The heavens will show us the way."

"What heavens? We're in a forest and I can't see a damn thing but your tension watch. None of your nodes or wrist straps have a flashlight by chance?"

"No. How would that help me optimize?"

"I've got a better idea," I say. "We get my car. Go back down—"

"I don't wanna go back down there. It's death there," Miami says.

"It's also where my car keys are. We sneak back in the cabin, grab them, and run for the car. Then we drive the Hell out of this town and call some real police."

"We could wait here until morning when it's safe," Miami says.

"Why would morning make it safe? The sun comes out, they see us when we see them. And they've got guns. Plus, who's to say they don't come looking for us before then?"

"It's not safe to go back there."

"It's not safe anywhere. But all hiding is doing is shredding my legs. And not in a good way. We stay here, we'll have ticks burrowing under our skin, infecting us with Lyme and all sorts of other diseases we've never heard of. Maybe there are snakes out here. Rabid squirrels. Poison oak. Deer with brain disease. If you haven't noticed, nature is the leading cause of death."

"Doctor says our blood is too strong for Lyme."

"No, Miami. Your blood is the same as everyone else's. No one is immune from Lyme disease," I say.

"I am. Mind over matter. I tell myself to act like I don't have it, refuse to believe I have it, then it goes away," Shane says. "Anyone can do it. Just takes commitment."

"OK, so you two aren't worried about ticks. What about the deranged rednecks who ran us into these woods? You don't think they'll come looking?"

"Yes, I am," Miami says. "But why go looking for trouble?"

"Right. Why leave the prickly blackness? I'm sure we'll be

totally fine here, wherever we are. I feel totally safe being blind. I bet the bramble is super nourishing, when you can get it down without shredding your throat. Deer ticks are probably 100 percent protein. And we can bite each other on the neck to refuel if we're going to continue to live under the delusion that Doctor didn't just make all that shit up."

"All honesty, Elips—" Shane starts.

"Val."

"Val. All honesty, I wanna get outta here too. I got the training to live out here for days, weeks maybe. I've eaten crickets—you're right about insect protein. But it's not ideal. And truth? A hyperbaric chamber does way more for my optimization metrics than this off-the-grid shit. I'm just hoping they'll forget about us and we'll get to the car in the morning when we can see."

A snap. Leaves crunch.

"What was that?" Miami asks.

"Sounds like it came from over there," Shane says.

No point in asking where "over there" is. It didn't come from right here, but we're not alone. Please be a deer. Even one with brain disease. Please be the maddest, sickest deer that ever lived. Just please, don't be one of them.

The sounds get louder. It's the even steps of a human or some other bi-ped creature walking. Bigfoot. Sasquatch. Let it be the Mothman. Silence. The creature has stopped. In the dark, if he can't hear us, we don't exist. The woods are silent. Black. Helen Keller's world. A blue glow. Subtle, but in a vacuum of sound and sight, the slightest light from a watch could be Polaris. Oh shit. Shane, you idiot. The paces begin again. Slow, deliberate. As Shane said, coming from over there.

"Run," I say. Hands in front of me, feeling for something that will hurt the rest of me worse, I run. Knees high, almost skipping. Someone that's not Shane or Miami is close behind, tearing through the brush. Don't look back. You can't see anything anyway. A scream. Miami. Is she captured? Stabbed? Or just scared? Whoever is behind me is getting closer.

Right foot, left foot. Shit! Hands out, break the fall. OK, that wasn't so bad. No, it is. The burning begins the moment my hands leave the brush. More blood. My knee throbs beneath the pants that must be more red than white by now. Not the eyes! It's instinct that squeezes them shut, not me. The light is so bright it blinds me with white as much as the darkness did with black. Blink them open. No, that's not right. That's a dead deer. Its glassy eye stares at me in the concentrated light of the flashlight. White worms—maggots!—crawl around its dead face.

A shotgun cocks. At least that's what it sounds like in the movies. And that's why the sheriff said we won't get far.

"I've got you dead to rights. Right in my sights." He'd sound tougher if it didn't rhyme. But also less deranged. Deranged like the rest of them. "And I've got you two, too."

The flashlight leaves my eyes and there are Miami and Shane, looking like deer in the headlights. Not just the startled expressions, but being about to die.

Shane's loose wires make him look like a robot in need of repair. Why didn't they run?

"Now, why don't you two step a little closer?" the man says. Oh, now they obey. "And you, get up off that dead animal." He doesn't have to tell me twice.

"Please sir, we just want to get out of here," Miami says.

"I'm sure you do, ma'am, but you're with that vampire cult, aren't you?"

"No! No we're not!" He points the flashlight back at me as I protest.

"If you're not with them, why are you dressed like them?"

"We were with them, but we're not anymore. We don't agree with what Doctor did either. And we don't want to bother you people or your town. We just want to leave and never come back."

"Well, I sure appreciate that, I do. That doctor and all you little vampires have been nothing but trouble since you arrived in town. Telling everyone that everything they do is killing them. That screaming shit in the middle of our town square. Bringing blood into the bars. If you people had just stayed here and minded your own business, we wouldn't be in this jam."

"I'm sorry. That sounds super disrespectful to your community. But the three of us, we just got here last night. That's why we're dressed in white. It means we're new. We just want to go home. Please."

"Now I'm sorry. I can't do that. I've got orders to bring you back down to the farm to talk to my commanding officer."

"Bro, you could just tell them we got away. We won't say anything. We'll just pretend we never met you."

"Would you lie to your commanding officer?"

"I'm an entrepreneur. I'm my own commanding officer."

"I'm not going to be able to do that. I'll be taking the three of you back down to the farm where my sheriff has instructed I take you."

"But if you take us back there, he'll kill us!"

"Yes, that is a possibility."

"So, don't take us there," Miami pleads.

"Now, honey, that's not an option. That would be disobeying a direct order from my superior. And what type of an officer would I be if I did that?"

"Who cares what type of officer it would make you? You'd be a good man!"

He looks at me, points the flashlight back in my face. I squint.

"Neither good man nor good officer disobeys his orders. Now, if you won't come peacefully, my sheriff says that my only other option is to shoot you all myself right here. He'd rather stick to Plan A, so I'd rather stick to Plan A."

"Both plans sound like death to me."

"Well, we'll just have to see what Sheriff says. Now, you three join hands and stand right in front of me and let's walk."

Chapter 11

Walking through the forest is easier with the beam of light from the deputy's—Arnie, he says, call me Arnie—flashlight. But it's even more unnerving with the rifle in my back. I'm pretty sure it's a rifle. I'm looking to make Director not hunter. To demonstrate his fairness, the affable Arnie lets us each have a turn with the barrel in our backs. What a guy. He's even listening to Miami babble in nervous terror without pulling the trigger.

"That's all it is really. It's about optimal vibrational energy levels. That's all we wanted from it. Self-enrichment. Energy is the key. All the bad stuff out there—drugs, pollution, junk food, stress, cable news—it all depletes energy. So the first step is eliminating all the energy robbers. Then we focus on attaining even higher energy levels. That's where the blood, sex, and yoga comes in. That's it. We just want energy. Not your town."

"That does seem like a noble goal," Arnie says.

I focus on the ground in front of me. It's exactly as I thought; bramble. A carpet of leaves, sticks, shrubs, and dead tree branches. So far, only one carcass.

"Yeah, you get it," Miami says. "We just want to be the best us. Live our best lives."

"Isn't that what everyone wants?" Arnie says. I'm not sure if that was supposed to be rhetorical.

"Well, some people have a strange way of showing it." Oh no. Shut up, Miami. Not the war. "So many people are just OK to consume toxin after toxin and never replenish the lost energy. Maybe they pop a pill and—"

"Why don't you just take us out of here and get a job at another station? You'd be a hero," I interrupt.

"Yeah, bro. I could hook you up. I've got clients on the force all over the country. I got them fit; they trust me. I put in a word for you, you're in."

"It's my sworn oath to protect and serve this community."

"Protect and serve by helping your psychopath sheriff murder innocent people?"

"You shouldn't speak of a great man like that," Arnie says, putting his gun in my back, putting me back in my place for opening my mouth. "He's brought our town back from the brink. You vampires aren't the first to suck the life out of the town. The opiates were worse. And Sheriff, he got them out, for the most part. Brought our little town back to life. We believe in that man. You'd be hard pressed to find a better man than that man."

"If you still need help with the opiates, I can get you in touch with ProWell Pharmaceuticals," Shane says. "Did some spon-con for them once and they've got this pill—Prolimia. Started as a weight-loss pill, but you give it to addicts with the Oxy, it'll make them puke it all up. They won't take the Oxy anymore since it makes them sick. It really works, bro. I got a contact there, good friend of mine. I can hook this whole town up!"

"Sheriff's way is working just fine."

Sheriff's way? Why does that sound like lowering the addiction rate by killing the addicts?

A snapping sound that I've gotten to know all too well as stepping on a dry, fallen branch. The rifle leaves my back. Arnie hears it too. Bang! A sharp pain in my ear. Was I shot? No, it was just the volume. The light beam goes wild, shining into the forest ceiling before settling on the floor. Turning around may be a bad idea, but it's instinct. The curious mind wants to see what's going on. The flashlight is on the ground. I grab it, scraping my hand on the thorny brush. Arnie is in the bramble, someone on top of him. I shine the light on the struggle. Tattoos. Shaved head. Phoenix. Rising from the ashes of defeat. He's got Arnie pinned on the ground. The rifle is a few feet away. Arnie is kicking. Shane jumps onto his legs. A cracking sound. Must be bone because dead trees don't scream. Phoenix presses his hands over Arnie's mouth and nose.

"I'll take my hands off and let you breathe, but if you scream or yell or wail or shout or fucking talk loud, I'll waste you right here. You see that blade on my belt? It goes right in your ear. Got it?" The blade is long enough to go in one ear and out the other.

Arnie appears to be nodding. It's the first time his face has been clear. He's young, probably barely older than me, but his hair is already receding. Maybe Shane will offer a discount code for a hair growth supplement or tell him how the right mindset prevents male pattern baldness.

Phoenix removes his hands from the smooth, shaved face. On the ground, wounded, the babyface deputy looks like one of the conscripted casualties of war.

"How many others are out here in the woods?" Phoenix asks.

It's quiet, just the normal sounds of the bugs and the slightest breeze rustling the trees. None of the sounds we've come to understand indicate the presence of another human.

"I'm not at liberty to say." Arnie gasps. He grimaces.

"Shane, why don't you break the other leg?" Phoenix says.

"Which one did I already break?"

"Fuck it, break either one. Pain is pain."

Shane raises his knee, foot positioned above Arnie's legs. I focus back on Phoenix's hands, pressing over Arnie's mouth, ready to muffle the imminent scream. Another crack. A muted wail. Arnie has to know he's not leaving this forest. No one is carrying the enemy. Is he thinking the same thing that Faylor and the others did when the gas filled the barn? Were they asking themselves whether Doctor and his prescription for a healthy life were worth dying for? Is Sheriff's mission worth dying for? What is worth dying for?

Arnie continues to moan and cry into Phoenix's hand. The toe of his left work boot is nearly touching his right shin. His ankle, beneath the khaki pants, must not be attached like it should be. I don't need to look away when I can leave the mangled legs in darkness.

"Hey! Turn that light back over here," Shane says. "I nearly tripped over—oh hey there." I point the light back on Shane. Wires dangling from his chest, he picks up the rifle from the ground. "I got our ticket out of here. Who's coming with me?" He turns and starts walking away, to somewhere, anywhere, rifle over his shoulder. Miami trails after him, immediately finding someone else to follow. Maybe she never needed a new name to signify her allegiance to whatever man could lead her out of her darkness.

"Shane! Where are you going?" Miami asks.

"Getting the fuck out of here with our protection."

"Not a good plan, man," Phoenix says. "Not without knowing how many more are out there."

"Right," Shane says, turning around. He lowers the rifle from his shoulder and uses it to beckon me. "Let's go, Val. We're gonna need some light and you're gonna need someone with a gun."

"What about your darkness training?"

"It didn't give me infrared vision. C'mon."

"How far you think you're gonna get on foot, Shane?" Phoenix asks.

"I did six nights of total darkness in the Nevada desert. My heart rate's down 5 bpm in the past few minutes and I had some blood and sex earlier. I'll be just fine."

"None of that matters to the copperheads," Phoenix says. "We're lucky as shit we haven't stumbled on any yet."

"Bullshit," Shane says.

"Copperheads?" Miami echoes. Her eyes dart to the ground, like saying their name will reveal they make up the entire forest floor. Like the snakes are writhing around in the leaves, wrapping themselves around her lean legs, and in a second, she'll be on the ground and they'll cover her body like quicksand.

"Yeah, they usually leave us humans alone. And we make a lot of noise when we come out here so they can hear us coming and hide. But you don't want to do that seeing how we don't want to alert any more deputies who might be out here to kill us."

Arnie moans. Like the idea of snakes added insult to his many injuries. Phoenix presses his hands harder on his mouth.

"So, what's your plan, bro?"

"My plan is to get the fuck out of these woods now that I found you all and get back down to the ranch with our weapons."

"We can leave in my car. The rifle gets us coverage to get to the cabin. It's on the edge anyway. I go in, grab the keys, and we're out," I say.

"That's a sound plan, Elpis," Phoenix says. Finally someone reasonable! "One last chance. How many more you got out here?" He eases his hands off Arnie's mouth, waiting for the answer.

"They're out he—"

The knife plunges into the side of Arnie's neck, ending his attempted scream. Phoenix thrust it like a shiv. The prisoner in him came out. The reasonable one. Oh, God. Blood spurts out with the velocity of a power washer. So much blood. So much life gone.

Phoenix yanks out the knife and jumps to his feet. The knife is back in his hip holster. His gray shorts are smeared with blood. Too much blood. I point the flashlight down. No snakes here. No corpses either. No wide, dead eyes. No shattered legs that look like an empty pair of khakis. No neck with a big hole in it.

"Fuck, man!"

I point the flashlight back up to Shane. Phoenix stands next to him, holding the rifle. His hands must have been as open as my mouth, watching the murder. The only thing Shane can't train for. The rifle at his side, tucked under his arm like he's an infantryman, Phoenix jogs into the darkness.

"C'mon. Follow me."

"Where are we going?" I ask.

"The cabin. Like you said. To get your keys. C'mon. Who knows how many of these fuckers are out here."

"And snakes," Miami says.

"Right. And snakes. Let's move."

The flashlight in my hand makes me important, a navigator of sorts. Don't let go. Keep it at all costs. Coach Trevor was right about grip strength. He said there were studies that indicated the greater the grip strength in old people, the lower the risk of death. Maybe it's true here too. The beam is pointed ahead, so we don't walk into tree branches and poke out our eyes so no light will save us. Or trip over deer carcasses or imaginary snakes.

Phoenix is a shit lead. The fact that Shane couldn't tell means he doesn't have the judgment to carry the gun. Miami too. They believe everything they hear. That's why they're here in the first place. They believed that the blood was the life, that sex and raw vegetables would bring them to a higher plane of existence. So, what does that make me? Stupid? Desperate? Frustrated that I wasn't achieving what I wanted? And where did that get me? Forging my own way through the darkness. And right back to following another bad man.

Miami and Shane are steps ahead of me in the beam of the flashlight, Phoenix a few paces ahead of them with the rifle over his shoulder and his finger near the trigger. If he's as good with the gun as he is with the knife, we'll be OK. For now.

Shane's guided navigation by stars must not have helped develop his internal compass. It feels like we've been walking for hours, covering much more distance than I possibly could have on my initial sprint into the woods. Whether Phoenix is any better remains to be seen.

The cayenne-filled Supersoaker is still at my side. There are many like it, but those are filled with harmless water, and this one is mine. Shane offered to carry it, feeling naked without the rifle he held for about ninety seconds. Relieve me of my double-fisting duties? Not a chance.

Ahead of us, Phoenix stops. He turns to the left, resumes his steps. And there it is, like an oasis in a desert: my Nissan Sentra in the clearing.

"Elpis, turn off the light." Blind again, I grab Phoenix's shoulders as I feel hands on my hips. Thank God for haunted houses or we may never have learned that behavior.

It takes everything in me—and the understanding that I don't have my keys tucked anywhere in my pocketless yoga pants—not to run to the car. Just one last stop and we'll be gunning the engine, driving as far out of here as the gas tank will take us.

The soft glow of the cabin light illuminates the scene just enough to find our way. Phoenix is a silhouette, a black shadow that hunkers forward on the edge of the forest. We're barely behind the last of the trees, crackling and crunching our way to the first cabin on the right. We've overshot our destination in the dark woods, wasted time. We should have been there by now. Maybe even on the way to my car. Stop thinking like that. This is the situation. Here and now. And we're getting closer to where we need to be. There's still light coming from the cabin. Royce's disregard for energy conservation, even if it is coming from a lantern, will come back to bite him.

No matter how much weight I cut, I'd never be able to squeeze through the tiny windows at the back of the cabin.

The farm is quiet, no murdering at the moment. The lumps on the ground are the only evidence that the farm is anything but idyllic. Six lumps. Unless one of the corpses got up and walked away, it's the same six lumps that were there when I fled. Bill, Lori, Kendall, Kinsey a.k.a. @lululunges, Faylor, and whatever Doctor's wife's real name was. The lights are on inside Doctor's house. A figure stands outside. A blade glints in the moonlight. Royce.

"I'll create a diversion. Elpis, you go through the front door. Shane and Harmonia, stay here and wait for Elpis to come back out," Phoenix says.

"I've gotta go in, too. My cellular gravitron is in there. That $7,000 piece of biohacking innovation was gifted to me. I'm not leaving it here. You don't let tech like that optimize the wrong people. That Royce asshole alters the gravitational field of his cells, he could be an unstoppable force of evil."

"Fine," Phoenix says.

"I'm not staying here alone with the snakes."

"There are no snakes, Miami," I say.

"I'll believe it when I see it."

"Maybe we all should have had that opinion before," I say.

"Huh?"

"You three ready?" Phoenix is bent over, like he's ready to press off a starting block.

"Yes."

Phoenix takes off along the forest edge. After a few seconds, the crunching of the leaves stops. Then Royce's voice.

"Where are you shooting from this time, bloodsucker?"

"Go."

Shane and Miami follow as we creep alongside the building. I peer around the corner. Royce is inspecting the arrow lodged in the ground about twenty feet from Doctor's shack. He raises the machete and saunters past the bodies to the barn. Wait. Be patient. Another arrow flies over the family of corpses, stabbing the earth. Royce jumps, turns so he's facing away from us. He waves the machete and walks toward the cabin previously occupied by some of the Grays now forever occupying the barn. Maybe he'll get lost in the field behind it. Probably not. We have to hurry. Miami and Shane follow my quick paces around the front of the cabin that just yesterday we treated like a palace.

Ow! I wince. Thankfully the pain in my big toe doesn't warrant more than that. Shane's stupid massage gun lays in front of my foot. I hop over it to the door.

My hand is on the latch. One squeeze closer to freedom. Shoving the door open feels like opening an escape hatch.

Inside, the lantern sits on the floor, emitting just enough light to almost miss the figures on the bed.

Chapter 12

Miami shrieks. Shane clamps his hand over her mouth, so it's just a chirp. It's OK. Medea—I can't even remember her real name!—rises from the bed. In her right hand, she clutches a knife. It's long with a curved blade, just like the one Phoenix carries. Maybe it's standard-issue with the gray attire.

"What are you doing here?" I think she says. Her whisper is almost inaudible behind the KN95 mask.

"We're getting my car keys and getting the hell out of here. You can come with us."

"Mentor and I are going nowhere. This is our home."

"You live in Cleveland," I say.

Maybe she opens her mouth to respond. We'll never know because Shane says, "Have you missed what's going on out there? They're on a murder spree. They've got guns and we don't."

"This is the war Doctor predicted," Medea says. "It's why we've been acquiring so much energy. To make a valiant stand and defeat the evil that is toxifying our world. When we stop the toxins, something beautiful grows."

"You're not defeating toxins here tonight. They've got guns," I say. "Please let me by so I can get my bag."

Medea doesn't budge. Her dark eyes stare into mine, the only part of her face visible.

"Fuck this," Shane says and starts to shove past the much smaller Medea.

"Mentor!"

With a sudden swiftness, Mentor pops up from the bed with a compound bow raised, pointed point blank at Shane.

"OK, OK, bro." Shane raises his hands over his head, international sign language for 'Don't shoot.' "Let's talk this through."

"Marig—Medea, please. They'll kill us," Miami pleads.

Marigold! Yes, that's her name. Marigold and . . . Banjo. I can see why they were so quick to adopt their aliases.

"Maybe," she says. "But Doctor said we never give up. This is our home that we've transformed into nirvana for energy. They will not poison us."

"Doctor's dead."

"Doctor never dies. His energy lives with all of us. It will live on forever and withstand the forces of evil."

"You don't need us to martyr yourselves. I'm gonna live forever. I'm not dying here," Shane says. He steps forward, toward the back wall where our bags are. Banjo pulls back on the bow. Shane stops.

"Medea, please let us go," Miami says. "We're not going to stop you from fighting. We just want to go home."

"If you don't fight the poison, you might as well be spreading it yourselves," Marigold says.

"They're all poison," I say. "I watched Phoenix murder a man in the woods. Doctor got a teenager pregnant."

"Whose side are you on, Elpis?" Marigold reaches her hand behind her back, so I clench mine on the Super Soaker.

"Neither. That's the point. You, Doctor, that sheriff—you're all diseased."

Marigold's arm moves quickly. Mine moves quicker. It's good to be an athlete. She raises the knife Norman Bates style and gets a load of cayenne pepper in the eyes. Blind, she stabs at air. Another squeeze of the trigger and Banjo's squeezing his eyes shut. Miami flails like one of those inflatable tube men at a car dealership. Shane pushes past her and tackles Marigold into the lower bunk, the one where I let Banjo grope me. Stupid. How did I fall for this? Am I that dumb? How did I not see it then? How did I let Doctor do the same thing?

Shane bashes the massage gun into Marigold's hand, knocking the knife to the floor behind the bed. Jesus, Shane. Why'd you have to pick that up? Just because it has gun in the name doesn't mean it does much as a weapon. Won't the psychos notice it's gone from outside?

Banjo's eyes are closed, but that doesn't stop him from pointing the bow at . . . well, no one for now. It's my opportunity to reach behind the bed. First my purse. It's comfortably over my shoulder with my hand inside, practically caressing my keys. Then the knife.

Shane has Marigold pinned, straddling her chest, pressing both hands down at her sides. The stupid massage gun is bouncing on the bed as Marigold continues to resist. Banjo's fingers are squeezed as tight on the bow as his eyes are shut. Can I get behind him and slice the string?

Marigold is kicking, but no matter how much yoga she's done, it's still physically impossible to kick or even knee Shane from that angle. It's like she thinks yoga can alter her anatomy. Like it could make up for ultra-long femurs in squatting. Never. Never again.

"Can you get me something to tie this bitch up?" Shane says.

"You're making a big mistake," Marigold says, breathing heavily. As I learned at the gym, physical activity makes it damn hard to breathe in a mask. "You're on the wrong side of history."

Shane releases his left hand and collapses the KN95 mask in on itself, shoving it into Marigold's mouth. She stops talking, but her hand is loose long enough to claw Shane's arm.

"Fuck!" That was too close to a shout for comfort.

"Shh."

"Don't shh me. That fucking hurt." His type O seeps slowly from his arm. He's trying to wrestle her arm back to the bed while still holding the other down. "Get me something to tie her up!"

Miami finally moves away from the door to Shane. She reaches over the bed and rips the nodes from his arm, then his chest. She holds the mess of wires. Marigold flaps her free arm, but it's too rhythmic and Shane catches onto the cadence. He anticipates her movement and slams her arm back on the bed. The veins in his forearms are popping as he lifts both her wrists and presses them together in front of her face. Her feet continue to kick the air and the white mask is starting to look a little wet in her mouth. Probably a lot of toxins in those fibers sitting on her tongue. That might even be as scary for her as being blinded and hogtied with a bunch of armed redneck lunatics outside. Shane holds her hands in prayer while Miami wraps the wires around her friend's wrists. As soon as they remove their grips, she chops down blindly on Miami's head.

"Ow!"

"Shh."

Banjo is pointing the crossbow around the room. Another shot in the eyes stops that.

"She won't stop moving!" Shane says. "Get me something for her feet."

With Banjo blind and the crossbow still for a moment, it's my chance to cut the string. I sneak past the suitcases, careful not to jostle them and let the blind man with the sharp object hear my movement. I'm almost behind him then, a second thought. Cutting the string castrates the weapon. What if we need it? Can months of strength training help me pry it from his grip? What about slicing him? Lightly. Only a flesh wound, letting the knife pierce only so deep to force his hand from the arrow?

"Get the feet!" Shane says. "I can't hold her forever."

"Well, what have we got here?" That obnoxious, half-drunken drawl. Locally hated. Only locally because he's never left this town.

We all stop and turn, even blinded Banjo. Royce has the door cracked open and he's peeping his head inside. A whooshing sound, then an arrow sails over his head and into the door. Not bad for shooting with your eyes closed, Banjo. It's enough for Royce to pause and for Shane to jump off the bed and grab his deep-tissue gun. His fingers are on the trigger, which is probably actually the start button. The bulbous end vibrates and spins and pulses at the end of the metal rod.

Royce steps into the cabin and Shane lunges at him. Royce doesn't have a chance to raise the machete at his side before Shane leaps, shoving him into the wall. Shane raises the deep-tissue massage gun to Royce's eye. The blood and the cry of pain, terror, horror, and dread all rolled into one give me no choice but to look away. A thud on the floor. The machete. More screams. More splattered blood. Droplets land on my cheek, my chest.

It's impossible not to steal a glimpse, just to make sure Royce is fully immobilized. His face is covered in blood. And it's not so much a face as it is a bowling ball. Does capsaicin still burn when the eyes are just two holes? One way to find out. The pepper stream enters the eye sockets like it should inflate a balloon at a carnival. Royce wails again, his hands to his face like the Munch painting. He's probably never seen it, probably never seen much art, never left this town to be hated elsewhere. Everyone must have looked like an invader to him.

Shane picks up the machete. He swings it, slicing a diagonal line through Royce's wife beater. The blood soaks through right away. Royce stumbles sideways. Shane knees him in the bleeding gut, sending Royce into the ajar door and tumbling out of the cabin into the dark grass.

Bad Vibrations

Blood-soaked weapons in each hand, Shane says, "Let's get the fuck outta here."

I shove the knife into my purse. The triple-layer cloth is enough to prevent it from stabbing me on the way to the car. Banjo gets another shot of pepper for good measure. He squeezes his eyes shut and grimaces, giving me the opportunity to snatch the bow from his hands. Stop doubting your strength! This isn't what you thought you were training for, but maybe it is. Miami grabs the arrows from the quiver on his back. Marigold is doing straight-leg sit-ups on the bed, her feet tied to the posts of the bunkbed with its white sheets now flecked with the red of Royce's blood. Her mask is spattered. She better hope it works as well as they say it does or she'll have real toxins to contend with.

Outside, Royce is writhing on his back, his grunts giving way to gurgles as his mouth fills with blood. Whatever. He's on the left with the rest of the death. To the right is freedom. I break into a sprint. The adrenaline overpowers the heavy-ass bow. There it is. The Nissan.

With arrows in both driver's side tires.

Fuck it. How much worse can it drive? You didn't have a wild shot, did you, Phoenix? You wanted us to stay here. You knew who was waiting for us in the cabin, and you thought they'd keep us. But, if they didn't, you'd need insurance, wouldn't you? You can keep shooting at me; I am not staying here to fight your war.

"What's going on out here?" Shari's nasal voice cuts through the darkness with all the smoothness of a steak knife in an operating room. "Royce?"

Let her find him. She deserves to see what's left of his face. I slide my hand around the knife to grab my keys. A press of the button on the key fob unlocks the doors. The single greatest invention for people in danger. After smartphones. Shane joins me in the front while Miami slides into the backseat. My finger is on the ignition button, my foot on the gas. Headlights flash on. Shari is running toward us.

"Go!" Shane shouts, like that wasn't the plan.

The engine revs and we're off. Sort of. The wheels grind on the gravel under the empty tires. To get to the street that brought us to this path barely wide enough for the Nissan, which appeared to be the town's main thoroughfare, would require a three-point turn.

There's no time for that. Not with Shari approaching, the gun drawn. To the vast unknown it is.

The gravel road winds around the farmland. How were they going to live come winter when the crops were out of season?

Oh.

They weren't.

They were going to take over more businesses in town, convert more acolytes, and get the grocer to carry organic, non-GMO, indigenous plants. This small farm wasn't the endgame. And that's smart on their part because it turns out all it takes is a sedan on bad tires veering right into the crops and a season's harvest is smashed and drenched in toxic exhaust. It's hard to tell when the driver's side of the car officially left the gravel since it sits several inches lower than the passenger side anyway.

"We're in the crops!" Miami screams from the backseat.

My hands and all the strength in my trained arms are turning the wheel, but the Nissan keeps drifting into the field, the rims scraping through soil while the tires stay on gravel. Shane grabs the wheel and the Nissan jerks partially back onto this poor excuse for a road.

Slow down. Apparently flat tires compromise steering. Take it slow. There is no one behind us. Shari with her flab squeezed into those khakis can't keep up with even a partially functioning car.

Bang. A thud behind me, like a bullet hitting the bumper. Just like that. Oh shit. The pedal is all the way on the floor. Fuck it. Shane will help me handle the vehicle again.

Another bang. And another. Louder. Closer. How many gunmen are there? My hands are at ten and two, but the car swerves anyway.

That second bang wasn't a gunshot; it was the rear tire.

The car careens off the gravel road and we're now totally in the field, mowing down the crops, killing the life fuel of the dead back at the ranch.

Miami screams again. Shane tries to grab the wheel as we head up a hill in the dark. Everything is a mystery in the darkness, even with the brights on. Out here, this field has the capacity for so much more darkness than even the crevices in the city where deer lurk. Light pollution is real. And may save a lot of lives. There's a wall of green in front of us. Shane tries to keep the wheel straight, but the Nissan swerves to the right and stops. My side of the car is somehow a full foot higher than Shane's now and my seatbelt holds me in, the only thing preventing me from defying gravity and holding some sort of side lever. We remain in this impossible arrangement for a second or so, in silence, like a breath will change the exception to the laws of physics existing in this moment in the car.

Stillness. Remain still. An isometric hold. The most important plank of your life. Shane is staring straight ahead into the illuminated tomato vines. What's going through his head? That he's getting his comeuppance for trying to use a movement for personal gain? Like me. Convincing the true believers—and myself—that I was one of them? Is it this lack of unity that left all of us—true believers or not—exposed? Punishment for remaining individuals when fealty to a movement means losing yourself for the greater good? Purgatory in this shitty sedan?

The car tilts. Shane's side smacks down, propelling my side up and up and up and holy shit, we're flipping. Hold on! To something! The wheel! Turn off the lights. If we can't see them, they can't see us. That is actually true in the rural darkness. The car rolls over itself again. We're upright now, on three rims and a tire. My hand has found the knob and the lights are off. Maybe they saw the uncontrolled beams and will assume we've rolled to our death. I kill the engine. The car is still. Miami stops screaming.

"Are you guys alive?" I ask.

"I've got ninety-three years left til my goal age. A couple flats won't stop me."

"Miami?"

"I think so," she says.

"The car is shot, bro."

"I know."

"Either of you know how to drive a tractor?" Shane asks.

"No."

"No."

"Me neither. But I've learned crazier shit."

"Where are we gonna get a tractor?"

"The storage shed right up there." Shane must be pointing, but I can't see him.

"Where is the flashlight?"

"It's somewhere over here. I saw it when we were flipping."

"No tractors. Marigold said everyone tills . . . with their hands."

Miami's voice is weak, soft. She breathes heavy. She must be terrified. "Maximum energy flow. No equi—"

"They do. Before you ladies arrived yesterday, I helped put some wheelbarrows back. It's filled with all sorts of machinery."

"And kerosene. That's where Doctor was sending me to get supplies to burn these maniacs."

"Then that's where we're going," Shane says. A thud. "Damn. My door's stuck."

My door opens, turning on the dome light and revealing the pepper gun by my feet. I grab it and step outside our temporary shelter.

"Miami, come on out." No response. The rear driver's side door opens easily.

Shane slithers out my door. "Shit. Where's the machete?"

"Here," Miami gasps.

The dome light illuminates all the blood in the back seat. Miami's whites are covered in it. The machete sits on her lap. With so much blood, it's hard to tell where it's all coming from.

"Where are you cut?" I ask.

"Everywhere," she says. "Take my energy. You need it."

"That's all bullshit. Blood doesn't give you energy."

"It sure takes it away," she whispers with a smile. "Take mine. Make me know it's worth it."

Shane pushes me from the door and wriggles into the backseat, next to Miami. He licks the blood from her cheek. "Doctor may be a rapist," he says. "But he had this right. I feel the energy already."

Chapter 13

"**Doctor had a** lot of good ideas that fucking work. Not the raping part, but the blood and the yoga. That shit's life-changing," Shane says as we walk through the darkness. Every so often I let go of one of Miami's legs to reach in my bag and switch on the flashlight—that had rattled its way around the Nissan and under Miami's feet—to make sure we're still headed toward the supply shed. Shane's no use in the lead since he's walking backward, his arms looped under Miami's shoulders. Every once in a while, she breathes.

"I bet you still watch Bill Cosby specials."

"His jokes are still funny. America's Dad. I thought."

"More like America's creepy uncle." The plastic gun shoved into my waistband is starting to put indentations in my skin.

"So you'll just write off any idea anyone had because they did something bad?"

Is Miami still breathing? I wait a moment to try to hear her before I respond.

"Do I think rapists should be role models? Oh, not just that, but people who actually tell us how to live our lives? No."

"So, everyone who committed some sex crimes, you'll throw out everything good they ever did? I gotta tell you, that's not gonna leave you much. You'll probably never watch a movie again. It's like you're throwing the good out with the bad. The baby with the bathwater."

"No, that's not what I'm saying. I'm willing to throw out all of Doctor's ideas because they were all just an elaborate scheme to rape teenagers. If he didn't convince people like you and me his way worked, he wouldn't have been able to convince someone like Lori who wasn't into wellness at all to bring her teenage daughter here." It took a lot of work to get that out. Carrying legs, even those as lean as Miami's, is hard.

"But they work," Shane says.

"You're not gonna live forever."

Suddenly, Miami's body becomes weightless. I take a step and my foot rams into her butt. Dropping her feet, I flick on the flashlight for just long enough to see Shane on the ground with an arrow sticking out of his chest. Of course. We're surrounded by enemies. Where's his heart? It doesn't matter since there's no beat. Another life cut short by the quest for immortality. Like Ponce de Leon. Icarus. That Nazi who drank from the wrong grail. Attempting eternal life is never choosing wisely.

The field is silent. Just the bugs fluttering or doing whatever it is they do. No labored breathing of someone maimed by a rogue machete. No defense of the cultural contributions of rapists. I'm alone. And it's not just freeing my hands of the corpse that is liberating.

It's time to run. The shed is my last chance. If my getaway is on a John Deere going seven miles per hour, so be it. Maybe the kerosene fire will distract everyone shooting bullets and arrows. A big fire that accelerates with all the energy of the crops and swallows the acolytes and this insane excuse for a local police department. Waco. Maybe the flames will spread to the woods and whoever gets stuck investigating this shitshow will need dental records to identify the body Phoenix left. Phoenix. He'll probably rise from the ashes and impale the CSIs with arrows from the sky.

Burn. It. Down.

For the second time since college, and the second time tonight, I break into a sprint. The water gun and my shoulder bag bumping against my hip may be slowing me down, but I'm not going for a record. I stop, filling my lungs with air. A sort of euphoria washes over me. It's more than having finally reached my destination; it's that runner's high. Endorphins. The real energy. The sense of accomplishment. A goal reached. The high I've been chasing. Maybe I need to lower my standards. Appreciate the little things.

Like finding the shed door unlocked.

I pull the cayenne-filled gun out of my pants and raise it in one hand like a gangsta. That'll actually work here considering it's plastic and the pepper water has no kickback. But what good is blinding someone in the dark? I reach into my purse with the other hand and feel around until I find the flashlight.

Let there be light.

Let there be accelerant.

A vehicle with an accelerator.

A weapons cache.

A prisoner?

He's tied to a metal shelf mounted on a wall. His eyes are bloodshot, but he sees me. The kid. The local. Dressed in white. The one who freaked out last night.

"You come to take more blood? I swear you got it all last time. The pills are out of my system."

"Who are you?"

"Eri— uh, Pelops." He smiles, but it's weak and it distorts the tattoo on his jaw.

"Your real name."

"Eric." He's skinny, everywhere but his face. The one thing that's consistent is the tattoos. They're tough to make out in just the beam of the flashlight, but they're all over his pale arms, neck, face, and the bit of chest peeking out of the tank top. The ones on his cheeks and forehead look like symbols. Chinese letters maybe?

"Why are you here?"

"You mean like in this shed? On this ranch? Or on this Earth? 'Cause fuck if I know that last one."

"The shed."

"Detoxing, yo. Doc caught me getting high again, so here I am, getting the bad blood out and the good blood in. You gonna give me some of yours? No one's been in for a minute. I'm feeling mad depleted, son."

"No. I'm here for the kerosene."

"Fuck, yo, why you need kerosene?"

"I need to set a fire." The space is cluttered with all manner of farm junk, probably left from the previous owner. It'll take a lot of looking with the flashlight. At least there are no windows. No one will see the glow of the beam. Though they may realize there are few other places I'd be hiding. I need to move fast.

"Aw, shit. You ain't a patient, now, is you? Fuck no, you're one of them. My dad send you? Burn us all down? That sounds like him. Fucking vigilante asshole. Fuck him and his fucking hat and his fucking fake-ass badge."

The hunt for the kerosene can wait.

"Your father? Who is your father?"

"Don't act like you don't know," he slurs with the drawl of a boy raised in a small town on the beats of the inner city. "He sent you here to burn out another doctor that made his town look bad. Same's he did to Doc Terry and her pills."

"Your father's the sheriff?"

"Pfft, he was. Until they fired his ass last week. Those deputies are next. They know it. Just a matter of time."

"He's not a sheriff?" Paradigms don't shift; they shatter.

"Bitch, why you playing dumb with me?"

"I'm not. Look how I'm dressed. Listen to how I talk. You think I know anything about your town?"

"Yeah, you're dressed like me. My old man may be a raging, psycho, fucking asshole, but he sure as shit ain't dumb. And he got Deputy Wade studying us. It'd be just like him to send some hot ho spy behind enemy lines."

"Maybe it would be more like him to send his own son."

He laughs. It turns into coughs. "Motherfucker, he did send me here. But not for no spying shit. Cocksucker wanted to get rid of me like he did all the others that got hooked on Doc Terry's pills. And now you're here to burn it all down, like her office. Don't matter none that Doctor's really doing the work my old man said he done."

"There's ketamine in the barn."

"Yeah, I know. They put it in the blood."

"You knew?"

"Fuck yeah, I knew. I'd know that shit anywhere. That's some easy shit to get from vets. The blood's cool and all, but the ketamine's what's getting me off the pills. Told you, Doc's really getting folks off drugs."

"Doctor's dead."

"No, he ain't his blood's magic. He can't die."

"When he loses all that blood 'cause some psycho ex-sheriff shoots him, he can."

"Aw shit, aw shit. My dad's here?"

"Yes. With some raging bitch named Shari and that idiot sycophant Wade."

"What are they doing here?"

"Well, they came looking for drugs and now they're killing everyone. Royce slashed Andromeda's throat. They shot up everyone in the barn."

"Doctor?"

"Dead. Last I saw they were closing in on him."

"Royce. You said Royce. Where's he?"

"Dead. We killed him with a massage gun."

He narrows his eyes. "So how're you still here?"

"Lucky, I guess. And I can run real fast." And I was never a true believer. Like when I got here, I'm in it for me. But he doesn't need to know that.

"You know why I'm here?"

"Your lunatic, homicidal father sent you here to get clean and probably punish you. You relapsed and this is Doctor's version of detox."

"Nah, that ain't it. I know why I'm here. I'm here to save ya'll. That's why Doctor called me Pelops. After my evil father cut me up into pieces and served me to the other Gods and shit, I went up to heaven and learned how to steer the divine chariot. I'll get us all out to Shangri La."

"Oh fuck."

"What, you don't believe me?"

"Look, Kanye, I've had a night from Hell. I watched a lot of people die. Not just die, get brutally murdered. My car's got three flats. Out there's a team of psychos impersonating cops and I've got some pill popper related to the lead murderer claiming to be the messiah."

"You got no car. You ain't from around here. And you got a water gun to fight your way out. Wouldn't anyone who could get you out of this place be a messiah?"

"Why would you help me? How can I trust you're not gonna run to daddy as soon as the arrows start flying? Oh yeah, cause Phoenix is out there shooting at us too."

"Bitch, how can I trust you? We may be dressed the same, but we're from different worlds."

I aim the flashlight around the room. What do kerosene jugs look like? Are they even jugs? Or bottles? Or some sort of keg?

"What's your plan?" I point the beam back at the scrawny kid. He can't be much out of his teens. How'd he have the time to accumulate all those tattoos?

"I lead you to salvation."

"Give me a play by play."

"Fine. First we need the arsenal."

"And where is that?"

"Look within yourself and you'll find it."

"What the fuck does that mean?"

"It means get that damn light out of my face and look for it. I ain't no arsenal!"

The shed makes me more uncomfortable the more I look around. It's like an episode of Hoarders or a secondhand shop with an inventory flow problem or a proprietor who maybe should be on the show.

"Can we ride out on the lawn mower?" I ask.

"Only if you want to make the biggest show of the slowest escape."

Bags of soil are stacked haphazardly against the wall. It's like they shoved all evidence of the drunken, destitute former owner in here. Beneath the apparent order of the cabins, the color-coded uniforms, and the regimented schedule is a foundation of disaster. A freezer full of hamburgers would, at this point, not be a surprise.

"You're getting colder," Eric says.

"You could tell me where this supposed arsenal is or at least what I should be looking for."

"You'll find it if you're serious about fighting your way out of here."

"I am serious. That's why I want it now."

"You can't commit to the search, how am I gonna trust you to carry it out?"

"Carry what out?"

"The mission for survival. Salvation."

"Again. Specifics!"

"You keep lookin' at me you ain't never gonna find the cache."

Rope hangs from what appears to be a nail on the wall. A tool chest is filled with tools that could be weapons. Any of them are a step up from a massage gun. A chainsaw dangles from a peg on the wall.

"Getting colder."

"I'm taking the chainsaw. We may need a massacre."

"It's heavy."

That's apparent. And it's awkward and now my hands are full and the flashlight just points at the dusty floor. Beneath a metal shelf containing enough toilet paper to survive a Chinese lockdown while on an American diet sit four jugs of kerosene. Yes. That's what the labels say. Four gallons.

"How the F did Doctor think I was going to carry all this?"

"He didn't want you to carry it. Something close to you will do that for you."

"Alright. Enough with the cryptic shit. I suppose the kerosene is your cross to bear. A job for the messiah."

"No. What good is kerosene in buckets?"

If it wasn't in my line of sight, this stupid game may have lasted forever. Or at least until Shari finally figures out that I didn't drop dead in the tomato plants. But there it is, leaning against the wall. The crossbow to end all crossbows. What looks like an umbrella stand filled with arrows next to it. The chainsaw can wait on the floor.

"The crossbow. That's it, isn't it."

"What crossbow?"

"That one!" Wild gesticulations in the general direction of the corner make my point.

"I don't see no crossbow."

"Are you blind?"

"No. I see a compound bow."

"Fuck your semantics. Subject-verb agreement eludes you, but you'll get snippy about a damn bow? This is it, right? The cache?"

"Yeah."

"And the arrows are going to carry the kerosene?"

"You untie me, yeah."

"Can you shoot?"

"Better than you."

"How do you know that?"

"I know it's a compound bow."

What is the appropriate level of concern about freeing a man who is so calm after being tied to a post in a dark shed for a day? Does he still not believe me? Or does he know something I don't? I mean, other than the difference between compound bows and crossbows. Maybe the drugs haven't left his system. Or he's steeled his nerves during face tattoo sessions.

"What are you planning to do with the compound bow?" I ask.

"Make them think it's a dragon attack."

"OK, that I understand, then what? How do we get out of here?"

"My old man—he drive down here?"

"Yes."

"We drive off in his ride."

"That requires keys."

"You've got a chainsaw."

"You can't hot wire a car with a chainsaw."

"Nah, homegirl, you can't. But you can use it to get keys off someone."

"I'd rather get out of here without confronting them. I saw what happened to Kinsey when she did."

"Either we confront them or we're on foot through the woods."

"I'm so sick of these people."

"You're sick of them? Try living with them for twenty years. Hip hop, chronic, tats—all the mark of the beast to them. And look at him now, out there doing the devil's business."

"OK, but the devil's got guns."

"You got a better plan?"

For all my education, I don't. The guy with the face tattoos has a better idea than I do. Problem solving, an essential skill of an account manager. Where did I get off thinking I'd earned Director status? "No. Flaming arrows and chainsaws it is."

"Then cut me loose."

With little diffusion of the beam, cutting tools are nowhere to be seen. Except . . . aha! The chainsaw! It's heavy. How could anyone chase you with this thing over his head? Forget massacring. Leatherface could have had a career in Strong Man competitions.

"Not with that! God damn, you are a crazy bitch. There's pruning shears or some shit around here somewhere."

Whether they're for pruning or trimming or topiary at the Overlook Hotel, a minute or so of fumbling in the dark earned me some sort of gardening scissors. They're big and heavy and a little rusty and they take both hands to cut the ropes tied around his hands and chest and the ones easy to miss at his ankles, but they get the job done.

"Boo!" He lunges at me. "Hah! You're sure jumpy ain't you?"

"I've only been shot at and held at gunpoint tonight."

"You'd think that'd put it in perspective. You wouldn't be scared of me."

"What I've learned tonight is that everyone is the enemy."

"No. Just them." Like he can see my face in the darkness, begging for clarification, he adds, "The people in this shit town, they just push their backwards bullshit. They keep killing everyone with their ignorance. They'll never wake up. They tried to kill me! So many fucking times. These people are evil and I'mma be happy as shit to watch them burn."

Well, the smoldering corpses will buy me a way out. Who cares about them?

Eric walks over to the compound bow. He counts the arrows in the umbrella stand. 1, 2, 3, 4, 5, 6, 7, 8, 9. He looks around, searching for something. Spastic, jerking movements like he's been tied up for so long he lost motor control.

"You see a quiver around here?" he asks.

Chapter 14

The going's slow, but we're making our way back to the cabin colony. It's more the nine arrows shoved into the waistband of my yoga pants that make each step so slow and deliberate. It's like being in half an iron maiden. Or some sort of medieval posture correction device. A barber-surgeon's cure for scoliosis. Shane probably tried something like this, maybe after reading about how slouching takes years off your life. Poor Shane. He may as well have been a true believer. They all wound up in the same place.

The chainsaw is getting heavier the farther we venture back through the field to the commune. The kerosene bottle in my other hand is much lighter, and the unbalance is making it a core challenge. Though I'm highly motivated to stay upright with the arrows at my back. Just stay upright and shuffle. Morticia Addams and her insane friend are on their way.

Eric holds the compound bow and another bottle of kerosene. Although the arrows will carry them most of the way like he said, we're lugging the bottles a lot farther than I'd anticipated. The rope that had tied him to the shed is draped around his neck. It's soaked in kerosene, as is Eric's white shirt. Maybe he'll remember to disrobe when the time comes to ignite the flames. Maybe he won't. Maybe I'll remind him. Maybe not.

Our current position in the field gives us the cover of darkness. They don't see our awkward approach anymore than they would if we were coming from the woods on the other side of the little colony where the lights illuminate them. Well, illuminate them enough to make them silhouettes. A shadowy figure paces near Doctor's house. Eric grabs my arm to stop me from getting any closer.

"Stay still," he whispers. An arrow slips out of my pants. What has my life come to? Please, whoever it is up there, let concealing arrows in my cult-issued yoga pants not be my last act on Earth.

The arrow's sharp tip is mostly covered by electrical tape. According to Eric, the tape adheres a rather elaborate network of cheesecloth, wire, and sparklers. Eric did not throw these together in the supply shed. Unless he was the one who left them like that in that umbrella stand, the arsenal for the war they expected, the blitz that came tonight. After jamming the girthy tip into the bottle of kerosene, Eric says my job is to ignite the arrow with the matches in my sports bra.

Eric mounts the arrow in the compound bow.

"Light it up," he whispers.

The first match is a dud. The second ignites, giving me just enough light to make out the tip of the warped arrowhead.

It doesn't light, but it feels like my hand might. The third match is the charm. The flame catches fast, so fast it almost catches my fingers then Eric's as he positions the arrow. Fingers to the flame, he launches it. The ball of fire flies through the darkness. Stay straight. No! Left! Maybe leaning to the left can cause the arrow to adjust courses. It never worked for bowling balls. Why do I think it would work now? And the rest of the arsenal adjusts course in my pants. Ugh.

We have one shot. If the fireball flames out, they know someone's shooting flaming arrows. They could hunt us down with their guns. Maybe we douse them in kerosene and fumble with matches in a panic and wind up throwing mini fireballs that also flame out before they pull their triggers.

The fire arrow disappears.

Either it didn't hit the barn or the gas that killed most of the cult wasn't flammable. Is there such a thing as a non-flammable deadly gas?

A glow emanates from the camp. It's not the explosion like we were naively hoping. The fire burns. We creep closer.

"What the fuck?" Shari shouts. "Hey Sheriff, you may wanna come out here. The bitch is on fire."

We're close enough to see, yes, holy shit, Lori is on fire. And there's nothing left to do but laugh.

"You literally missed the broad side of a barn."

"Well, I hit the broad on the side of the barn."

This makes me laugh harder. I shouldn't have judged Eric for the dated urban slang or the face tattoos or that he was so deep into the doomsday plot he thought he had a savior role; that was damn clever.

Shari puzzles over the flaming corpse. *After all this, how stupid would it be if my hiccups revealed our location?*

"Sheriff's busy with their leader, Shari."

"Lori's on fire. He may wanna come out here."

"So what?" Wade says. "She's dead."

"In my experience, corpses don't just ignite."

"All the corpses you meet at happy hour?"

"Fuck you. Like a vacuum repairman knows fuckall about bodies."

"I know corpses release gas. And these cultists out here with their raw food diet are likely filled with a lot of gas. Maybe it's that spontaneous *convulsion*."

"Or we ain't alone out here, you moron. Get Sheriff."

"You wanna be a real deputy, make your case why this matter merits the big man's attention."

The stupidity of evil. How much of what we describe as evil is just stupid people trying to do smart people things? How many nefarious cabals are marred by incompetence and petty bickering among henchmen? You catch them when they don't think anyone is watching and it's a middle school cafeteria. How many evil deeds are performed by people too stupid to realize they're doing the wrong thing?

"What's this look like to you?" Shari asks, standing next to the fiery cadaver. "She wasn't impaled last time you saw her, was she?"

"Not that I recall."

"Don't it look like one of those cult arrows?"

"Now that you mention it."

"Go get Sheriff."

Wade retreats toward Doctor's ramshackle house. *That's our signal.* Eric pulls back on the bow. This arrow, without its fire, hits the barn. Shari pulls her gun.

"I know you're out there, you crazy cult motherfuckers!"

Another arrow in the bow. Another wild shot.

Shari's figured out where they're coming from. Gun drawn, she starts heading our direction. She doesn't see us in the corn, not yet.

She's invisible in the darkness of the cornfield. The sounds of rustling in the crops are getting closer and closer. She's even violent toward plants. Crunch, crunch. More corn children never to grow to meet a grill. Be still. Please, Eric, don't—

The arrow slides out of my pants. The stalks rustle. Not the death rattle like Shari brings, but just enough for a lunatic plant destroyer with a gun to confirm that she was right; someone is out here. She comes at us quickly, crunching and swishing and she's upon us. She's still just a darker shade of black. A shadow upon a shadow. Death incarnate. Her hot mouth breath hits my face and there's no time to think. Pull the trigger. She screams.

I flick on the flashlight. The gun is now just in one hand. She's rubbing her eyes with the other. Until Eric plunges the arrow into her shoulder like it's a knife. She shrieks. Angry, not scared. The gun falls into the corn.

Screw the Super Soaker. The pepper gun can go in the waistband that will never stay up again. Shari's pistol can be pried from my cold, dead hand. It's heavy. Doctor was right. What was I thinking trying to be a powerlifter?

"Hi, Shari, you hateful bitch," Eric says. "Oh you think you're gonna win? My dad ain't gonna save you."

"You've always been a miserable shit, Eric. I ain't surprised you wound up here with these freaks. You deserve each other."

She stops talking. She's not so confident when she feels the cold gun barrel in her temple.

"I'll give you one chance. You got a working car here?" The words just spill out from me. So easy like a Stanford experiment. When the tables have turned, you hear yourself becoming a villain. Or would be the villain without the context of how the rest of the night has gone.

"No. You idiots shot out the tires."

It's not worth telling her we're not those idiots. Next question. Who's the fake cop now? "Why are you still here?"

"We're making sure every last one of you is dead. This is our town and it's gonna be cult free. We'll stay here all night if we have to."

"Where's your leader?" I ask.

"With yours," Shari spits.

"Doctor? Where is he?" Eric asks, vulnerable for the first time tonight, without the confidence when he was tied to a post in a dark shed.

"He's in his house, the one he stole from my friend, giving Sheriff a whole lotta that energy."

Eric drops the bleeding bitch into the corn and tears through the crops toward the cabin colony.

"What are you doing?"

"I gotta save Doctor!"

"Shit."

Shari thrashes in the corn. A kick to some part of her body—possibly the chest, at least that's what it feels like—sends her back. The gun is in my hand. I pull the flashlight out of my bag with the other. She's on her back, trying to catch her breath from what must have been a heel to the solar plexus. They say recoil is a lot more intense in real life than in the movies and a gun is tough to control with one hand, even for people who have, say, handled one before.

Screw it. Not worth the risk. It'll be steel knuckles.

The butt of the gun to the skull sends Shari back again and she's tangled in the corn. 1, 2, 3. No rustling. No movement. Unconscious. The flashlight back in the bag, it's time to move. Upright with the rest of the scoliosis-correcting arrows, the gun in my hand and my finger off the trigger so it doesn't blow after a trip on a cornstalk. How the fuck do you turn on the safety? What is the safety? It should be more obvious. Run slowly, anathema to a sprinter and anyone fleeing for her life.

Eric is already standing in the empty space between Doctor's house and the cabins. His compound bow is ready to fire. At what? Well, that remains to be seen. What remains of the posse has yet to be seen, or to see us.

"You got the gun?" Eric asks.

"Yes."

"Shoot it."

"At what?"

"Anything."

"No."

"No?"

"I'm not wasting a bullet. And I don't know how to shoot it anyway. I'll probably wind up killing you. Like one of those kids who gets into his dad's gun safe."

"Fine. Gimme a match then."

"OK." He yanks the pack from me as soon as it's out of my bra. He walks to Loris's smoldering corpse. Poor woman. Not even mommie dearest deserves that. He pulls the arrow out of her abdomen. Maybe that's more dignified. The flame is extinguished. He lights it again.

"Douse the door," he says, nodding to the kerosene bottle he salvaged in our corn tussle.

"The plan didn't work," I say. "But we got here anyway. There's no need to give twenty families closed casket funerals."

"Not the barn. Doctor's door."

So he's cool with torching Doctor all of a sudden? Best not to mention it. Maybe he'll remember his surrogate father is in there, not just his real one.

How much kerosene does one need to light a house on fire? The answer will have to be the whole jug. Most splashes on the door, but the surrounding area, even the bay window, gets a sprinkle.

"Move," Eric hisses.

With the flaming arrow in the bow on his shoulder, it would be stupid of me not to do as he says. The arrow hits just above the doorknob. The flames spread fast.

"Goddammit! Grab him, Deputy!" Sheriff shouts from inside the house.

The flames are burning a hole in the door. The knob falls to the ground and rolls toward Kinsey's bloody corpse. The wood smolders. The fire is already burning out. Maybe torching Doctor wasn't the plan, but there are easier ways to get a man's attention. We could have yelled, "We're out here! Ve vant to drink your blood!" And saved the kerosene to douse the sheriff then shoot him up with flaming arrows. We're out of kerosene, but the fireball could ignite his polyester uniform. Though we've lost the element of surprise that we have fire.

The weakened door splinters under the force of the sheriff's foot. What's left of the wood that hasn't been consumed by flames crashes to the ground. Out walks the sheriff, surrounded by flames. His gun is in his hand. Shari's gun is in my hand. Only one of us knows how to use it. The bad one.

He storms out of the house, through a gate of flames. He blinks the smoke out of his eyes. Behind him, the moron deputy drags Doctor onto the stoop elevated by a simple concrete step. He's weak, bloody, hanging onto his last drops of energy.

"Put down the piece, old man," Eric says, his bow raised, the string pulled pack, his father in the crosshairs.

"Boy, what the Hell are you doing with that thing? That dope convince you you know how to aim?"

"No, Dad. Doctor did. He got me clean, too. No drugs, see." He nods his head at his arm that's holding the bow, like his father could possibly see track marks or none in the darkness. "All just good energy."

"This rapist?"

"This savior. He saved me when you couldn't."

"He didn't cure you. He's a con man. A parasite like the rest of those folks promising to make your pain go away. Nothing can cure you. That's why you're here, for the final solution to our parasite problem."

"Fuck you! I'm no parasite." Eric pulls back on the string. It squeaks.

"You didn't let me finish. You're my son. So I'll take you home. And we'll try something else to—"

Wade shrieks as Doctor lunges at him. "He's got my gun!"

The gun is limp in Doctor's energy-depleted hand. Who is he trying to point it at? He looks confused. Old. Wide-eyed, hair springing wildly from the low ponytail. He didn't come here thinking he'd be in a Mexican standoff, even though he engineered the circumstances that created one.

Everyone is still.

Then Wade says, "Now, why don't you hand me that gun back?"

Doctor looks around at the sheriff aiming at him, at Eric with his bow on the sheriff, and at me aiming my gun at Wade because no one else is. He flips the gun under his chin and BANG. Doctor's body hits the ground. A final twitch, the energy stolen from teenage girls and countless vulnerable women looking for a better version of themselves goes back into the ether. The ether deserves it more.

"Shit. Who'd have thought the last thing he'd do would be the first thing I'd respect him for?" the sheriff says. "He should have done that years ago. Before he even got weak idiots like you believing in his sorcery."

"I don't believe it!" It just comes out of me. Why do I feel the need to defend myself to this lunatic? Maybe it's me who needs to believe that I don't believe. That I'm still me. That no part of me will spread the gospel of this religion back in Pittsburgh until my neighbors decide the only way to protect themselves from its viral load is with guns. No, that's not me. Live and let live. Or die. What do I care what they do?

"You don't believe it then why are you here?"

"To be better. His philosophy may be a bunch of bullshit to fuck teenagers, but his lessons taught discipline. And I've got it now. And I know my goals."

"Your goals? And what are those?"

"To get out of here and live happily ever after." Saying it out loud feels good. Aiming the gun at his head feels better.

"You really oughta put that down," the sheriff says.

"No."

"Don't point that at Sheriff!" Wade shouts.

"Put it down, Valerie. You don't get to kill him," Eric says.

"I reckon you want that job," the sheriff says.

"You're sure as shit right," Eric says, closing his left eye as his right looks through the scope of the bow. I point my gun back at Wade. As much as he might fancy himself his sheriff's keeper, everybody still has some sense of self-preservation.

"You know we did every goddamn thing for you and this is how you turn out. Everything. And it didn't matter. You just had to find all those parasites. First the hip-hip and the drugs and the low-life friends. Then there's a goddamn cult and a charlatan for a leader who comes to our town and steals land from my old friend and leeches off—"

An arrow plunges into the ground mere feet from the sheriff. Eric's is still in the bow. A coup failed. But some troops are still alive.

"Always more of you. Just when I think you're all exterminated. Like the roaches you are, you just keep coming back."

"I've got 'em, Sheriff!" Shari is sprinting toward us from the cornfield.

"You've got nowhere to go," Sheriff shouts. "Come on out. You'll never hit me from that distance. Amateurs."

"Give me your gun, Wade," Shari says between heavy breaths as she reaches our little standoff.

"Fuck you, Shari. Sheriff needs me."

"You spend as much time handling that gun as the one in your pants, maybe I'd trust you to hit something."

"Reveal yourselves!" the sheriff shouts.

"Not you, Wade," Shari says.

"I wasn't gonna, you bitch. I'm no pervert like that doctor."

"Let's get it over with," the sheriff bellows. "Better you come to us now than we come to you."

"Yeah, how's that been going for you?" Shari says. "Give me the gun."

"Just come out. You don't have much hiding time left. Don't make things worse for yourselves."

Oh shit. It's tomorrow. Wade's face wasn't coming into focus because I've been pointing my gun at it for so long; it's because the sun is coming up. The thinning hair, the slightly too large ears that maybe hair once covered—it's all clearer now, even more so than when he first arrived in his hat yesterday. Shari, her blond hair pulled back so tight she gives herself a discount facelift. It's all the more exaggerated by the blush contouring where she thinks her cheekbones are. Who gets all made up for a massacre?

And the sheriff. The slight paunch of the stomach not quite testing the tensile strength of the thread holding the buttons. Did he ever officially wear that uniform? It fits like it was issued twenty years ago to a fitter man who spent more time on himself and less time fixated on elements of the town he didn't like.

Three locals in stolen uniforms with guns drawn. Losers. LARPers, holding onto power that was stripped away.

"Alright, we're here. But don't try anything, you diseased pigs." Marigold and Banjo approach, dressed in their gray uniforms, bows out, arrows pointed. Marigold's mask is back on, protecting herself from the unclean population and their droplets that pack more death than a bullet.

Banjo's eyes seem to have recovered as he points his arrow at Shari. Marigold points hers at Wade. Eric and his father have each other in their crosshairs. My gun is back at my side because the isometric hold is tiring and I'm re-evaluating who I want to shoot.

Will it be Marigold before she makes this situation worse, like she did every other since I've met her two days ago? Or will it be Banjo for following along like her stupid dog? Or Wade for being the sheriff's dog? Or Shari because she's most likely to kill me? Sheriff for starting this shit? Or his son who isn't going to be as useful when the sun finishes rising?

If only this gun had enough bullets for all of them. Wait—how many bullets does this gun have?

"Now, this can go one of two ways," the sheriff says.

"Bullshit, Pop. You see how many weapons we've got here? There's an assload of ways this shit can go down."

"And there's that mouth again. I raised you better than that, boy."

"Gimme the gun, Wade," Shari says.

"No ma'am. I'm protecting my sheriff."

"Only way you'll protect him's being a human shield. That's all you're good for."

"You wouldn't have had intel on these cultists without me."

"That don't mean you know how to shoot a gun."

"Just on account of my vision don't mean I can't hit the backside of a broad!"

"Broad side of a barn, you idiot. And you couldn't hit it. Not in any way could you hit that."

He's not the only one.

"Will one of you point the gun at that coward in a mask?" the sheriff says.

"Coward? Just because you don't believe in science doesn't make people who do cowards," Marigold says. "You call me a coward now, but I'm not the one whose insides are rusting. And I got you in my sights. Who's the coward now?"

"Sheriff, if this fool would give me the gun, I'd point it at her in a heartbeat."

"You are a coward. Hiding behind your snake oil salesman. His energy healing isn't real. And deep down, you know it. Who's denying science now?"

"Do either of you know what science is?" It's an explosion. Good thing it's my mouth, not my trigger finger.

"Elpis, shut the fuck up," Marigold says. "Whose side are you on anyway?"

"I'm on no one's side. I just don't want to die here!"

"Well, that's too bad," the sheriff says. "'Cause I'm damn willing to give my life to make sure you people, you plague on our town, are exterminated. So, go ahead. Keep talking your nonsense. Shoot me. You're all gonna go to wherever your Hell is."

"They don't believe in Hell from my research, Sheriff. They don't need it as they think they'll live forever in these bodies or in the earth," Wade says.

And it just takes that few seconds of sycophantic rambling to let his guard down. Shari grabs the gun and BANG, a shot into the ground. Arrows plunge into Shari's chest. She drops. Sheriff squeezes the trigger. Another bang. It's concussive, even in this open air. Marigold's gray mask turns red. She tumbles. Banjo's arrow sinks into the sheriff's leg. He squeezes the trigger again, but he staggers and the bullet misses everyone in this little circle of death. Wade pries the gun from Shari's corpse grip and aims it at Banjo.

"Don't you dare try to refill your *quaver*."

"Don't need to, man. Your dear leader's dead."

"Not from a leg shot. I studied you people and your weapons. Arrows to legs don't kill no one. That ain't a lethal shot."

"Man, you don't know us. You did, you'd know we sometimes dip our arrows in snake venom."

The sheriff drops, rolling onto his back as he hits the ground, convulsing. His legs kick, his eyes open wide. Foam erupts from his mouth. He goes still, eyes remaining open.

Chapter 15

Wade places his fingers on the sheriff's neck. He shakes his head. Back on his feet, he raises his gun, aims it at Banjo.

Eric fires first, but bullets are faster. The recoil sends Wade into enough of a backbend that the arrow Eric dutifully aimed for his head whizzes past. Banjo shouts and grabs his thigh where the bullet hit. The only reason Wade manages a face shot with his second bullet is because Banjo is already collapsing forward. He trains his gun on Eric, who reaches into his quiver for more ammo.

"Put down the gun," I say, pointing mine at Wade. I must look like I know how to use it because he immediately drops his and sprints for the woods like he's, well, me a couple hours ago. I let him go. What else could I do? Throw the gun at him?

The blood is pooling on Shari's chest. Her uniform, which the rising sun finally reveals to be less a uniform and more a Wal-Mart brand button-down tucked into slacks vaguely the color of the sheriff's. Well, the parts of his that aren't soaked in blood.

And then there were two. Eric stands over his father's body. He sweeps his hand over the dead man's eyes. With his eyes closed, he looks almost at peace. Eric doesn't.

"I'm sorry for your loss."

"He was an asshole, but he was my dad."

He'll be missed. Not by anyone I know.

"Doctor was more of a father to me than he ever was," Eric says. "Got me clean. Got me clean again. Accepted me." Eric walks the few feet to Doctor's corpse with its hole through the skull. He brushes aside bits of skull, brain, and whatever tissue litters the face to close Doctor's eyes that are miraculously still intact.

Two men dead before their bodies wanted to go, yet lived too long.

It's time to leave.

"Where are you going?"

"Back to town. Find the real police," I shout over my shoulder.

"You ain't gonna grieve and shit?"

"I'll grieve on my way. Walking Shiva."

"The fuck's that?"

"Nevermind. How long will it take to walk back to town?"

"Hour maybe. A little less. Unless someone picks us up."

"Who's gonna pick us up like this?" Heavily armed. Blood spattered all over our white uniforms. We look like vigilante yogis. Which is what we are.

"I know everyone 'round these parts."

"And they know you."

"What's that mean?"

"When I got here, the first thing the first person I met asked me is if I was here for the cult. They know you. They know you're part of it. They cool with picking you up?"

"Yeah. They know me."

We start walking down the middle of the street, like the double yellow line is our yellow brick road. We're off to see someone, anyone. Hopefully someone who can tell we're not the problem and can get me home because clicking my heels sure as shit isn't working. And give me a brain that will make sure I never, ever listen to an Instagram influencer again.

The road winds up a hill, leaving our destination a mystery beyond the horizon. Vacant land populated with some sort of indigenous yellow-flowered weed nearly the height of the corn stalks as far as the eye can see to our left, the woods and its corpses to our right. How many bodies will they drag out of the bramble? Who that still walks among us could lead them to the fake deputy beneath the trees? Will anything be left? And what of the massacre on the farm? It makes Jonestown look tranquil. If only it had been Kool-Aid. But, ugh, the sugar content.

We walk in silence. There's nothing to say. He doesn't seem to want to kill me, and at this point, what else do I need to know?

No sounds but our feet on the pavement. Heavy steps. It's been a long night. Good thing we had the energy transfusions. Shit! Stop thinking like that! There is no energy. But why does it work? Why am I still walking after being awake for almost twenty-four hours? Adrenaline? Wait—what time is it? My phone! 5:43 a.m. But that doesn't matter. What does is the two bars. Finally. Service. Civilization. A lifeline.

"Stop!"

"Why?"

"I'm calling the police."

"Why?"

"Why? To come get us and see if anyone is alive on the ranch! If my car didn't run off the road, I wouldn't have found you. Who knows who else is hidden in some shack somewhere out there, bleeding to death."

"OK. But you better tell 'em you're with me. If anyone even picks up."

"If anyone picks up? They're the police!"

"It's early. And they cover four townships."

It's ringing. Cuts out, then rings again.

"9-1-1. What's your emergency?"

"Hello? Oh, thank God. There's been a massacre down on this ranch."

"A what, miss?" The operator sounds like a nice lady, someone who takes her kids to church every Sunday and cuts the crust off their PB&J. Who knows what kind of monsters she's creating.

"A murder! So many murders! Please get someone out here fast. Some people could still be alive!"

"Where are you?"

Shit! She cut out. Maybe the other side of the street has better reception.

"I'm, I'm not sure. We started at the diner, then took a long, winding, rocky road." A little help here? Eric doesn't take the hint from my imploring gaze. "Eric, where are we?"

"Route 119," he says.

"Route 119."

"What township, dear?"

"What township?"

"Unity."

"You're joking."

"No, it's Unity."

"Unity."

"You're just on the road? Are you in a vehicle?" she asks with such patience. She doesn't assume I'm in a cult.

"No, we're on foot. Please —"

Something, someone snatches the phone out of my hand. Deputy Wade races into the center of the road. He stops, taps my phone, disconnects the call.

"Give it back, asshole."

"Now, that's no way to talk to your new friend."

"New friend? You tried to kill us." Eric raises the compound bow. "What's stopping me from killing you?"

"Now, you know I didn't hurt no one back there. Never raised my weapon at you until you raised it at me. I got nothing against you folk. I was just doing my job."

"Your job is vacuum repair," Eric says.

"By day. By night I'm a volunteer deputy, sworn to protect."

"Why don't I shoot you?"

"Give me back my phone." Now he's got a gun pointed at him, too.

"Now, just a minute. I got an offer for you. Quick pro quo."

"Quid pro quo."

"Nah, this is like a pro quo done fast. Like this: you don't shoot me and I *carburetor* your side of the story, I tell the cops we came down and Sheriff, Shari, and Royce killed everyone."

"So, you're offering to tell the truth. Why would we need that? We can tell the truth."

"Well, you've got Shari's gun and those bullets will be a match to at least some of your friends back there. Who's to say you didn't pull the trigger?"

"How can we trust you?" Eric asks.

An arrow falls at his feet. The gun may be new to me, but the instinct to raise it must be evolutionary. To raise it at anyone, everyone. At Eric who does the same with his compound bow, jerking his head, desperately seeking the source of the arrow. Even raising it at Wade, who definitely did not fire. And we can all point our weapons at a single target as Phoenix emerges from the yellow weeds.

"Where's this motley crew headed?" he asks, pulling another arrow from his quiver.

"We're leaving."

"I don't think so," he says.

"What's there to stay for? Doctor's dead. Everyone is dead."

"They're only dead if we let them be dead," Phoenix says. "We rebuild. On their remains. Our soil will be filled with their energy and our harvest will be the most abundant the world has ever seen."

"That's not how it works in in the twenty-first century," I say. "It's a crime scene."

"So?"

"Yeah, it still legally belongs to Doctor," Eric says.

"Doctor is dead. The dead can't have possessions."

"What was his is bestowed to his children," Phoenix says. "Us."

"We can rebuild," Eric says.

"Huzzah!" Wade raises his fist in the air.

"The first energy transfer is coming from you," Phoenix says. "We'll take all the energy you've got."

"Whatever you need," Wade says.

"This guy." Phoenix snorts. "Let's go. Back to the ranch."

"No. There's nothing but death there."

"All the more reason to bring it back to life. It'll rise again, like Phoenix out of the ashes."

"There are no ashes. It's all blood."

"And the blood is the life," Phoenix says. He's staring at me, his eyes wide. He raises his hand that holds the arrow. He lifts his knee, like some tribal dance. "The blood is the life. The blood is the life. The blood is the life." He stomps and waves to the rhythm of his words.

"The blood is the life," Eric says. "The blood is the life."

They chant in unison, waving and stomping and tapping their bows on the ground. "The blood is the life. The blood is the life."

"The blood is the life," Wade says. "The blood is the life." Without the aid of a percussion weapon, he claps his hands and alternates his foot stomps to sync with the others.

They face me, forming a circle around me, surrounding me, closing in. Tapping and stomping and chanting, "The blood is the life."

"Say it," Phoenix says.

"No."

"Say it. The blood is the life. It's so easy. Just say it," Eric says.

"No."

"Say it, Elpis."

"The blood is the life. The blood is the life. The blood is the life."

"Say it."

"No!"

And the instinct, some innate, primal urge that we must have developed somewhere along the line when we learned the greatest threats aren't to the body but to the mind, takes over. It's like someone else is raising the gun and pointing it at Phoenix and pulling the trigger. But when the bullet leaves the chamber and Eric falls to the ground, gut shot and bleeding, it becomes clear it was me who shot. It turns out I wouldn't be able to hit the broad side of a barn either.

"I didn't want to take you by force. That always makes things a lot more difficult. But you're not giving me a choice." Phoenix raises the crossbow. He angles it down at my leg.

I'm not going to die today. It will be worse. Debilitation. Disability. Doing his bidding. He won't pretend his sex cult has a lofty goal.

"No. Put it down so we can help him."

"Fuck!" Eric screams. Blood seeps through his white shirt and between his fingers that are trying to hold his innards in. "Why'd you shoot me?"

Wade presses his hands over Eric's hemorrhaging gut. He fumbles around, unsure of where to put his hands. That's why real deputies get training.

It was an accident. That would be the truth. The guilt almost pushes it out of my mouth. But that would make the gun in my hands, pointed at Phoenix's face even less of a threat than he already believes.

"You think I'm a doctor just cause I followed one for a long time? I'm no doctor. I can't fix him. We got enough blood for the life."

Wade leaps to his feet, his red right and left hands yanking Eric's bow from the ground. He rams it, arrow first, into Phoenix's back.

The arrow burst through his abdomen, tearing through the gray, ribbed fabric, flinging pieces of skin and muscle onto my destroyed yoga pants. Phoenix grasps at the arrow, but the blood flowing from his gut soaks his hands and he can't get a grip. He falls to his knees, tries to speak, but only a gurgle comes out, like he's choking on his own blood, his own life. He keels forward, his face hits the asphalt. The crossbow holds onto the arrow and sticks out of his back like a stegosaurus.

Eric wails, shivers, and his head falls back. The two bleeding men on the ground lay still, silent.

Bad Vibrations

Wade throws his hands in the air. "It was self-defense! All of it."

"It was. That's the truth."

"My offer still stands."

I nod. The gun goes into my bag. For now.

And we walk to salvation, leaving bloody footprints on this road paved by what those men insisted were good intentions.

Acknowledgments

Thanks to Marc and Joe at Blood Bound for believing in this crazy project when I first mentioned it last year. Knowing it would have a home motivated me to finish what I started during lockdown after we'd all been set free again.

My beta readers—Richy, Wendy, and Sarah—were all indispensable as always. The final manuscript is far better due to your input.

Thank you to Benj for sitting through the tedious NXIUM documentary with me as I researched this book. I can name three worse movies off the top of my head you agreed to see in theaters with me.

And, of course, the parents. You've been encouraging me to write my horror stories since you installed Monsters & Make-Believe on the family computer when I was five. Someday I hope to write an epic about "horrible heads."

About the Author

Lucy Leitner is an advertising writer and award-winning journalist in Pittsburgh, PA.

Her transgressive fiction includes the novels *Outrage Level 10* and *Working Stiffs,* as well as several shorter works that appear in anthologies and Godless.com original series.

Printed in Great Britain
by Amazon

35683556R00081